STICK AND STONE

EXPLORE AND MORE

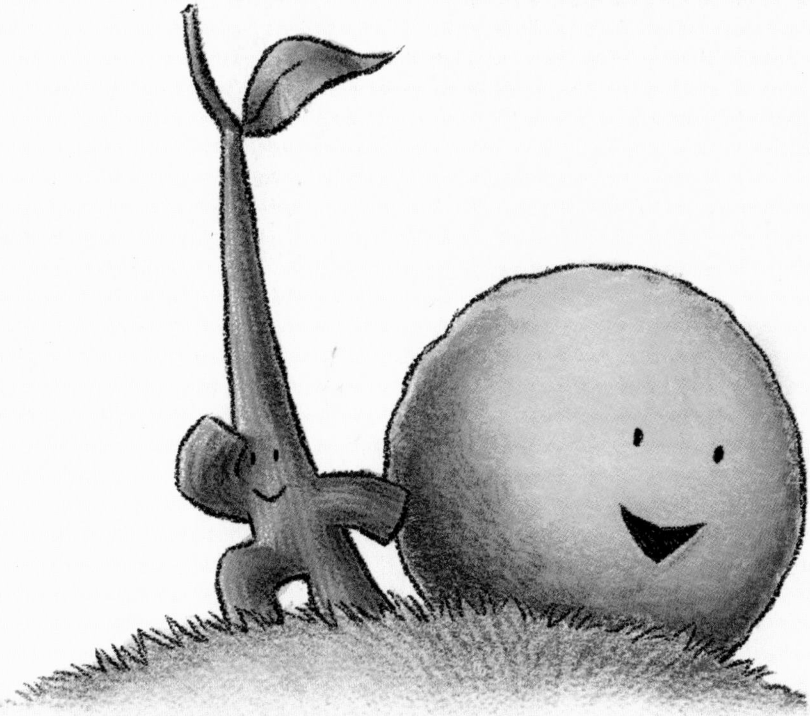

BETH FERRY

KRISTEN CELLA

CLARION BOOKS

Imprints of HARPERCOLLINS*Publishers*

HARPER alley

CONTENTS

STICK AND STONE
AND THE NATURE GIRL

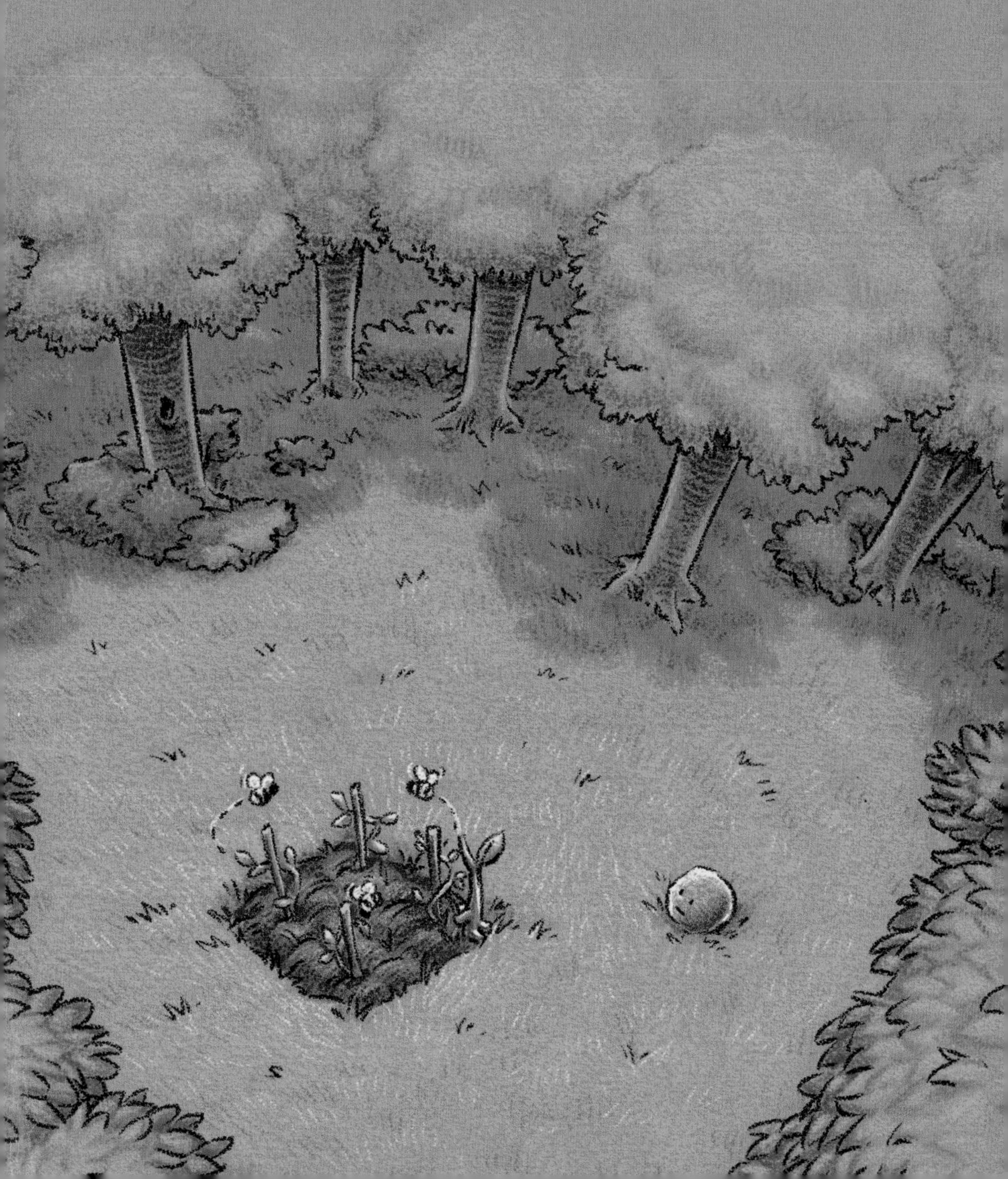

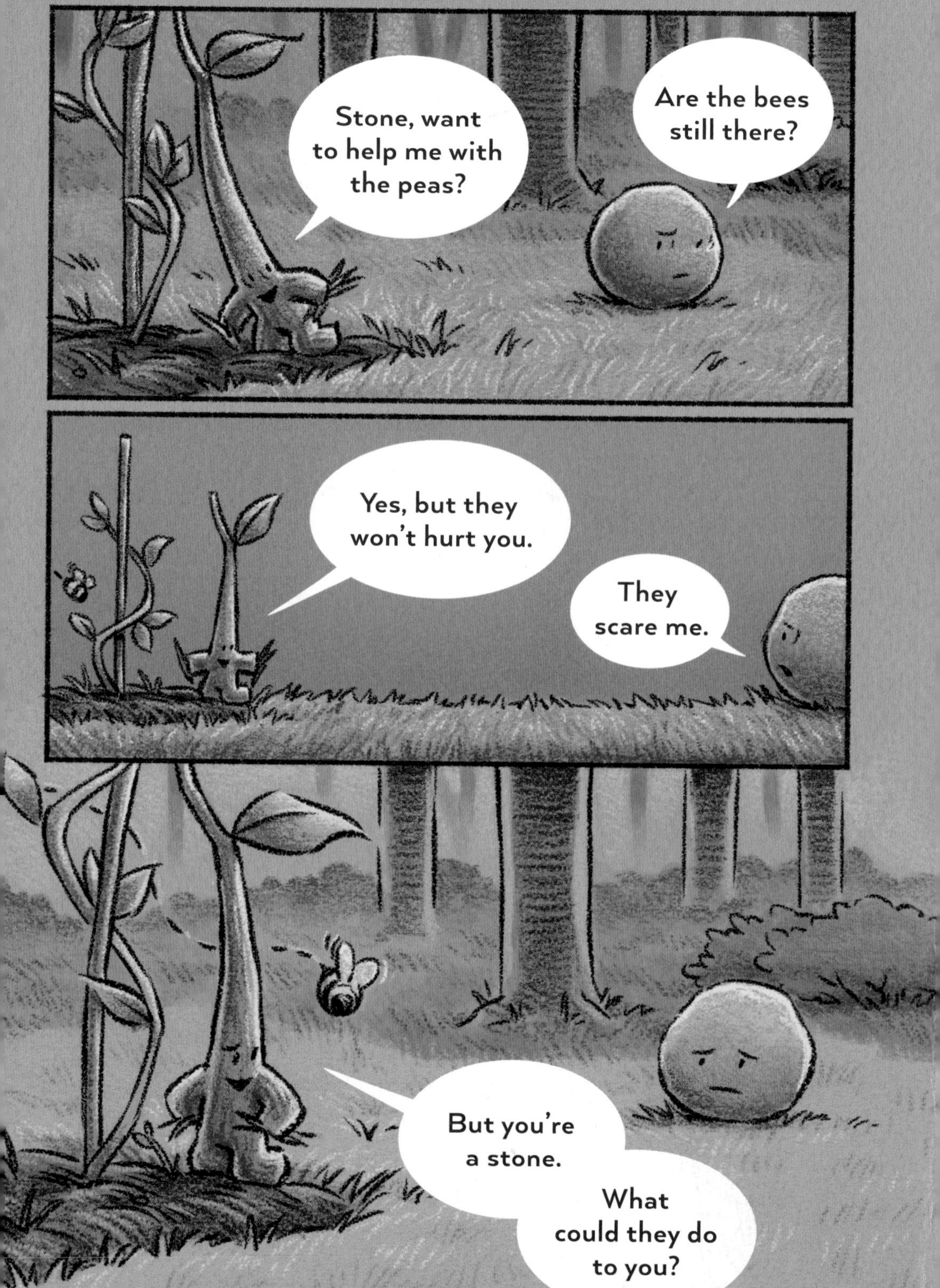
Stone, want to help me with the peas?
Are the bees still there?
Yes, but they won't hurt you.
They scare me.
But you're a stone.
What could they do to you?

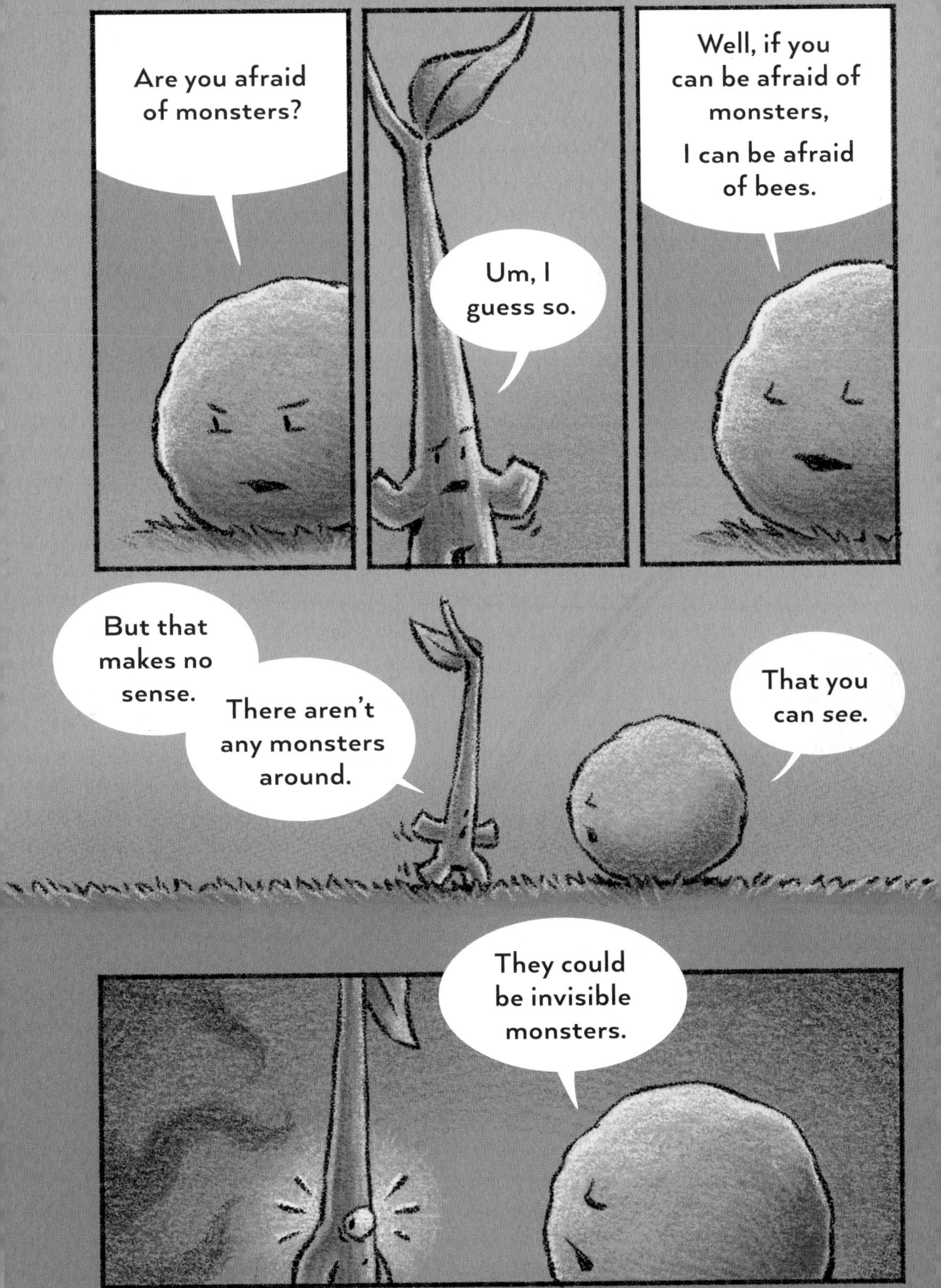
Are you afraid of monsters?
Um, I guess so.
Well, if you can be afraid of monsters,
I can be afraid of bees.
But that makes no sense.
There aren't any monsters around.
That you can *see*.
They could be invisible monsters.

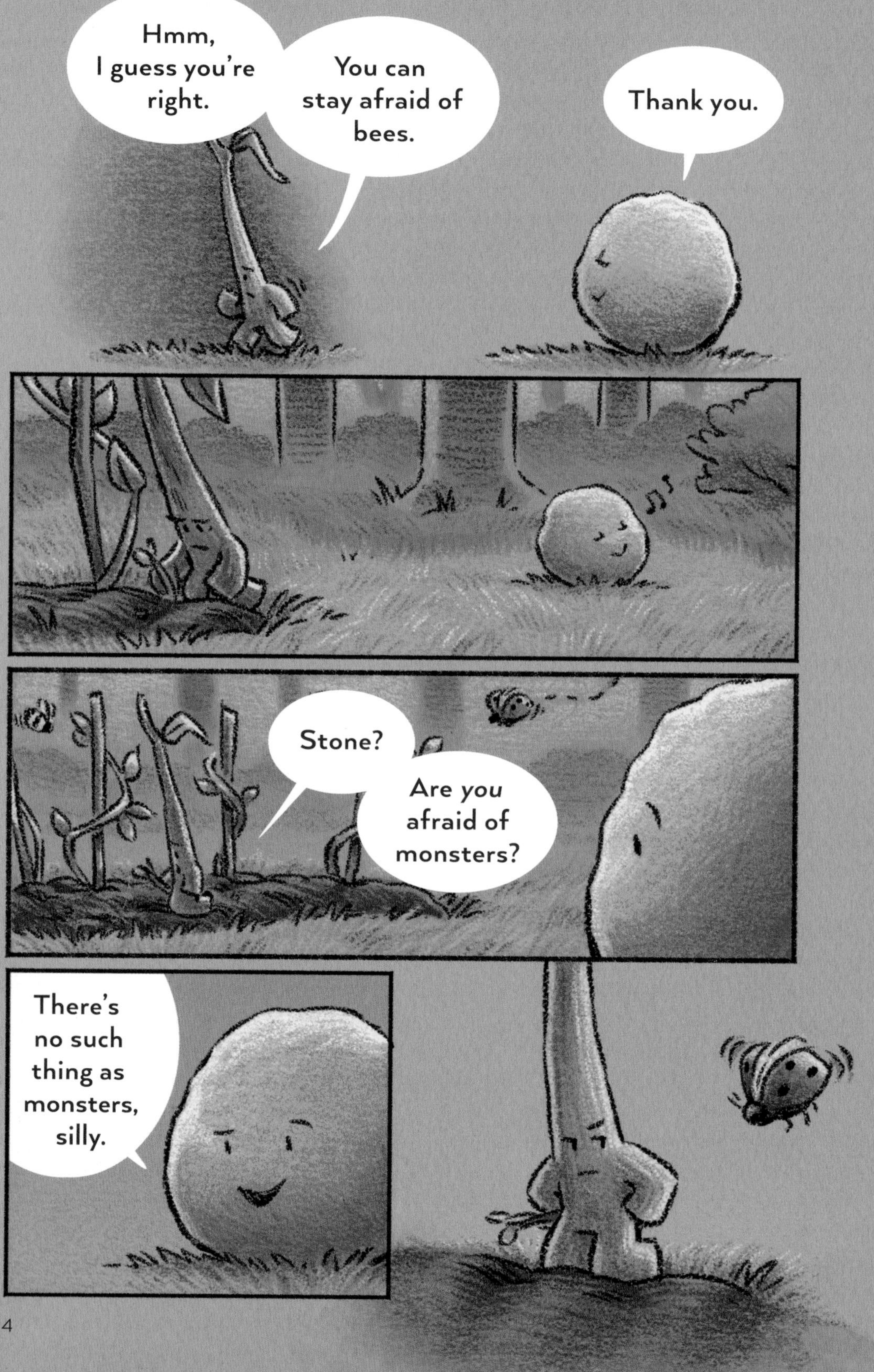

Hmm, I guess you're right.
You can stay afraid of bees.
Thank you.
Stone?
Are *you* afraid of monsters?
There's no such thing as monsters, silly.

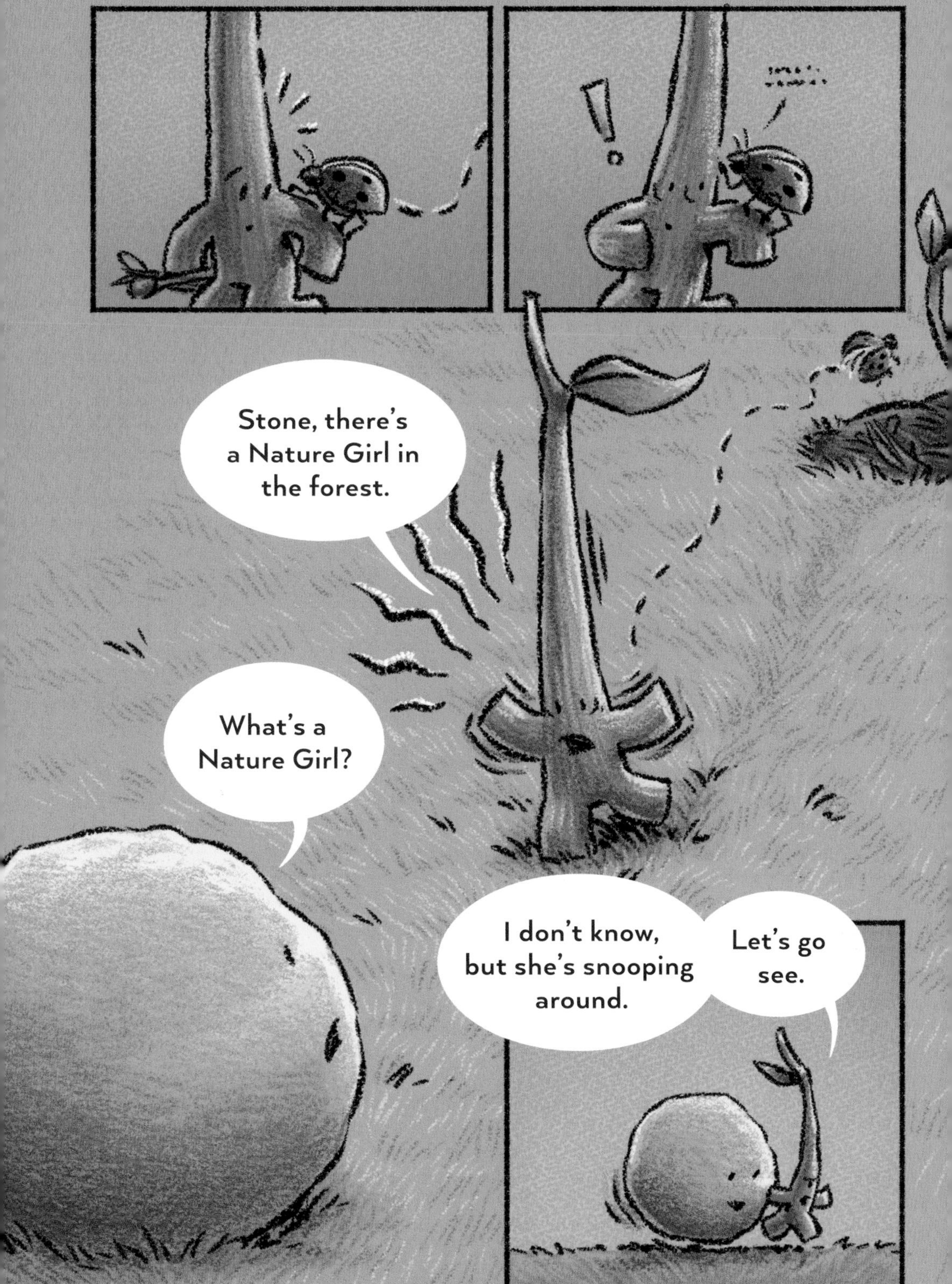

!
Stone, there's
a Nature Girl in
the forest.
What's a
Nature Girl?
I don't know,
but she's snooping
around.
Let's go
see.

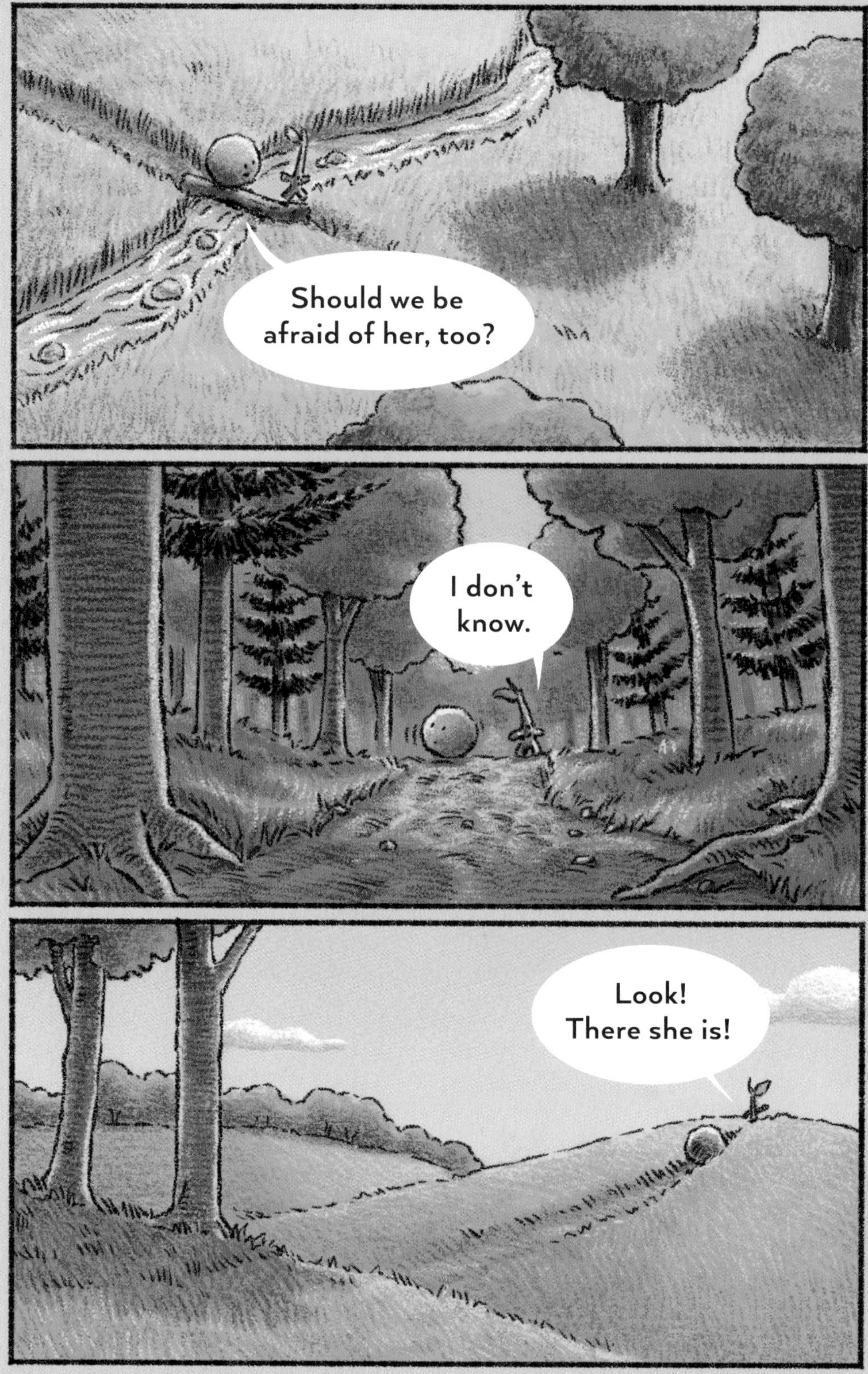
Should we be afraid of her, too?
I don't know.
Look! There she is!

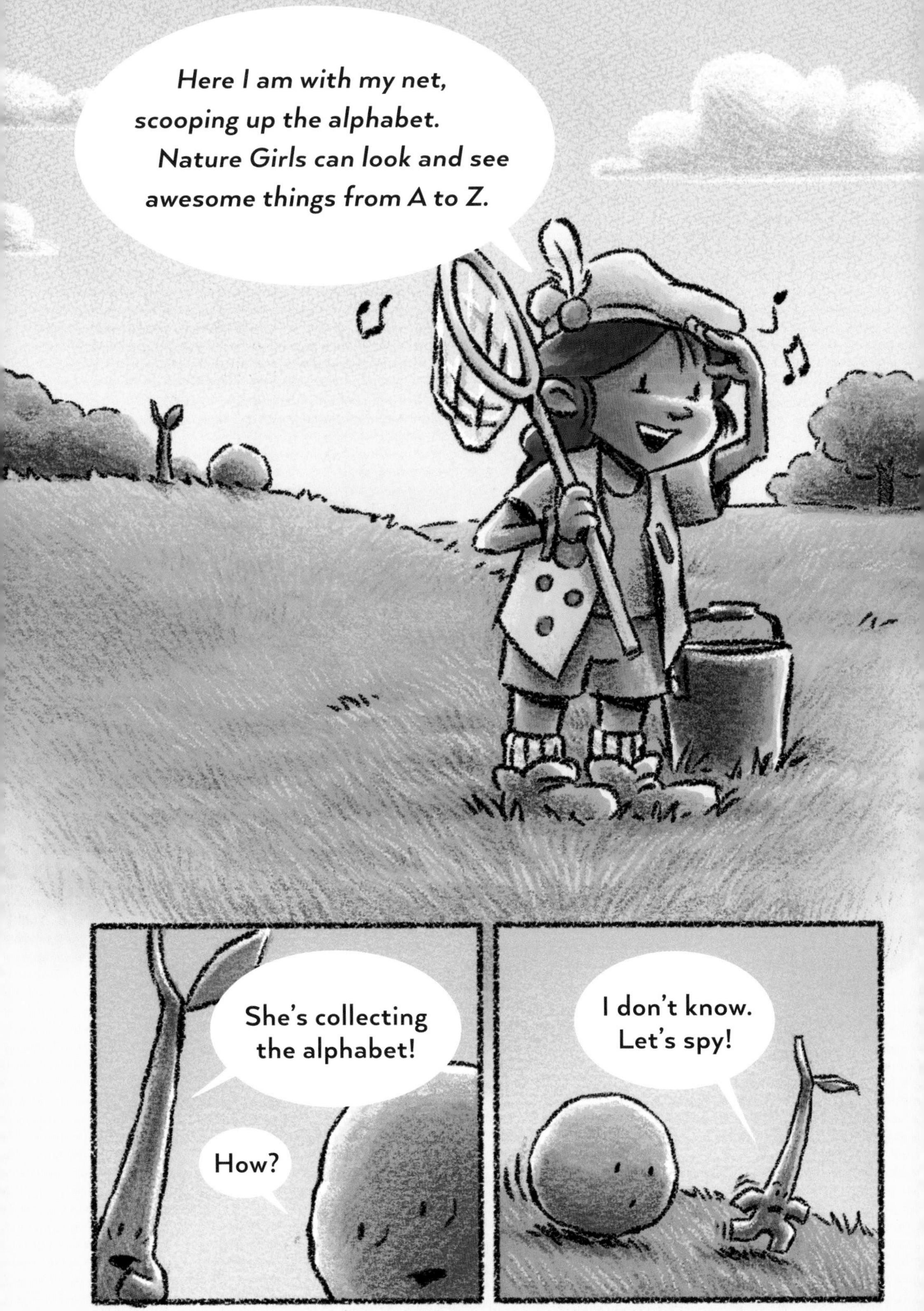
Here I am with my net, scooping up the alphabet. Nature Girls can look and see awesome things from A to Z.
She's collecting the alphabet!
How?
I don't know. Let's spy!

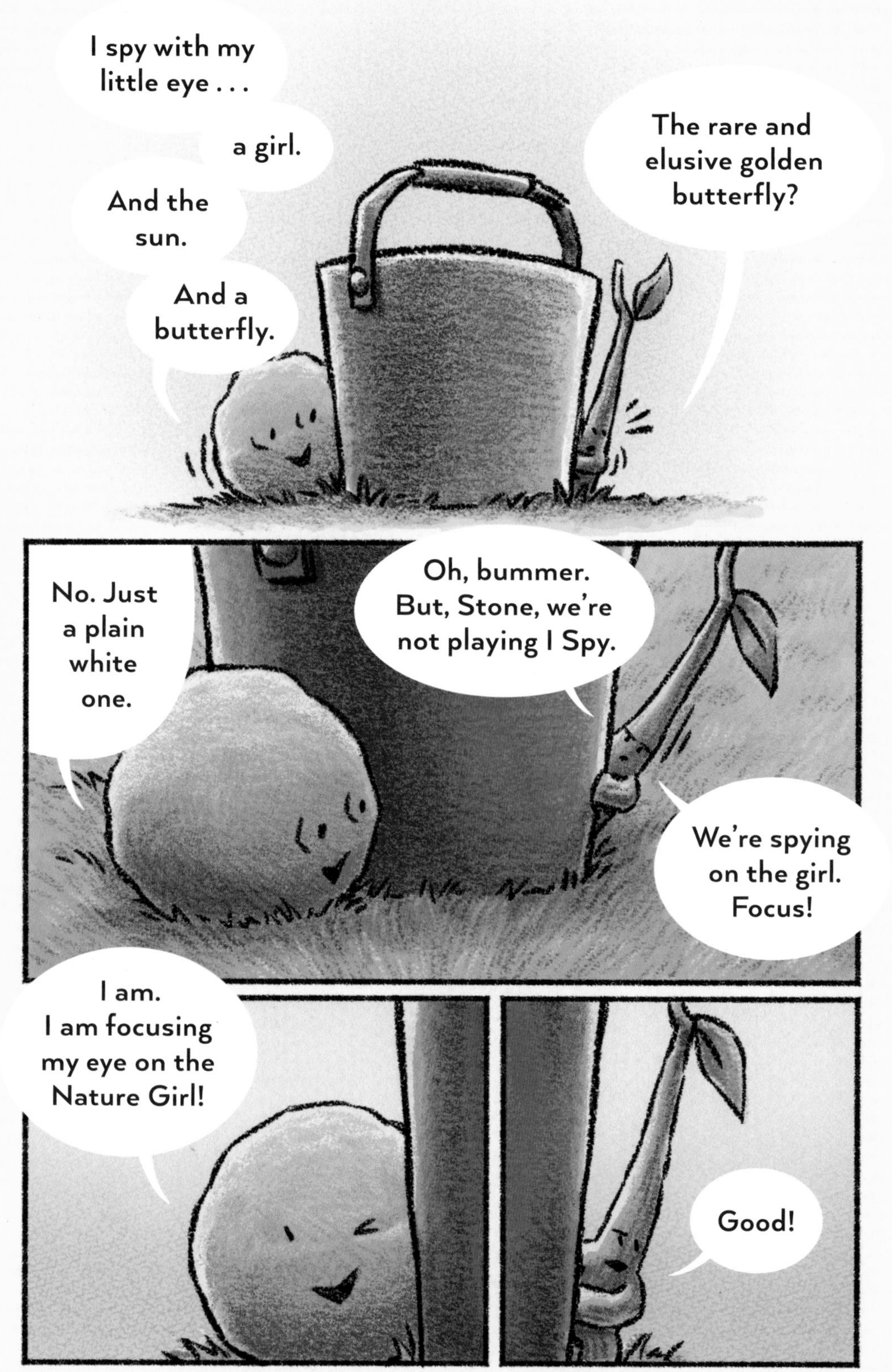
I spy with my little eye . . .
a girl.
And the sun.
And a butterfly.
The rare and elusive golden butterfly?
No. Just a plain white one.
Oh, bummer. But, Stone, we're not playing I Spy.
We're spying on the girl. Focus!
I am. I am focusing my eye on the Nature Girl!
Good!

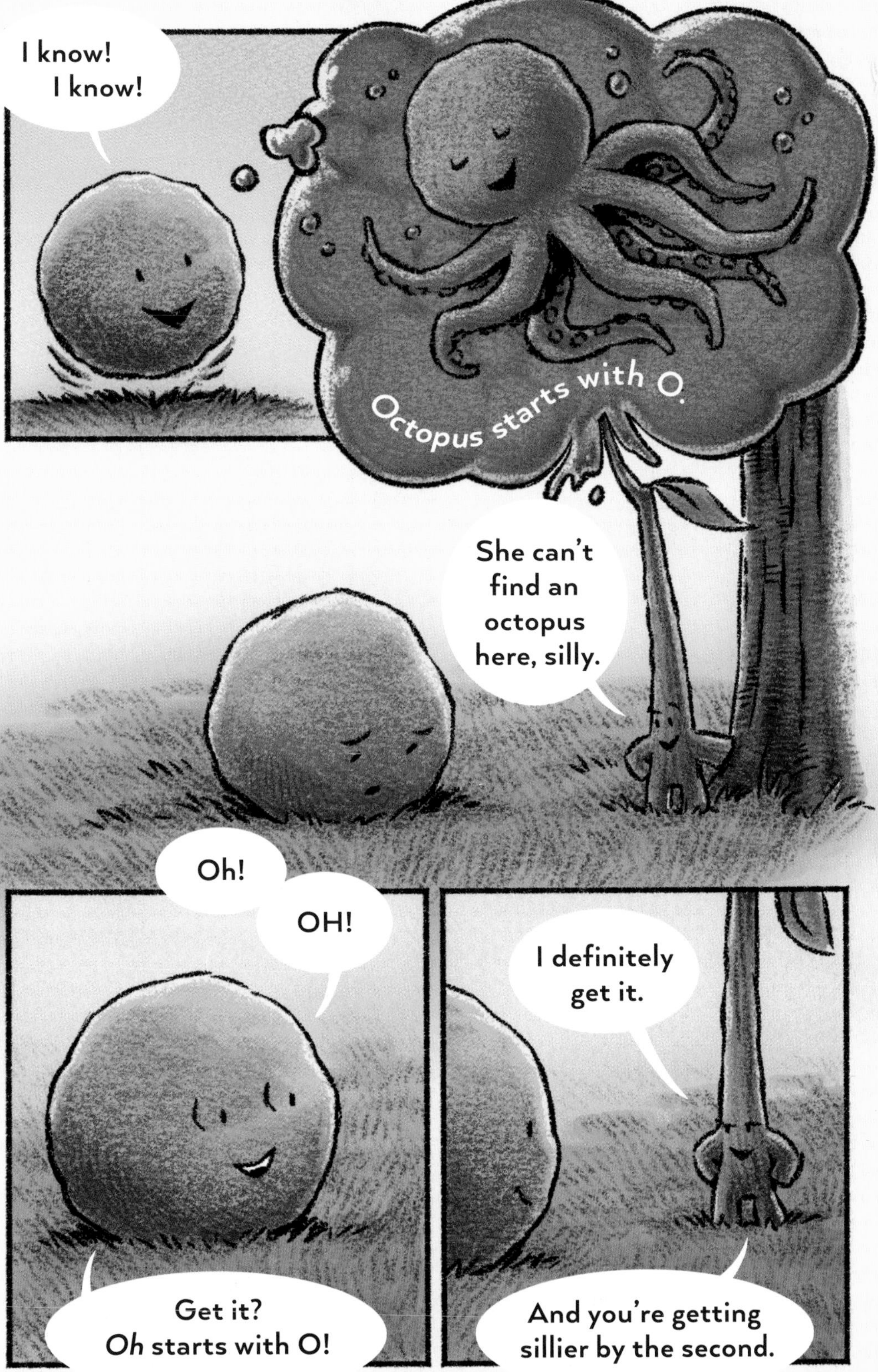
I know! I know!
Octopus starts with O.
She can't find an octopus here, silly.
Oh!
OH!
Get it? *Oh* starts with O!
I definitely get it.
And you're getting sillier by the second.

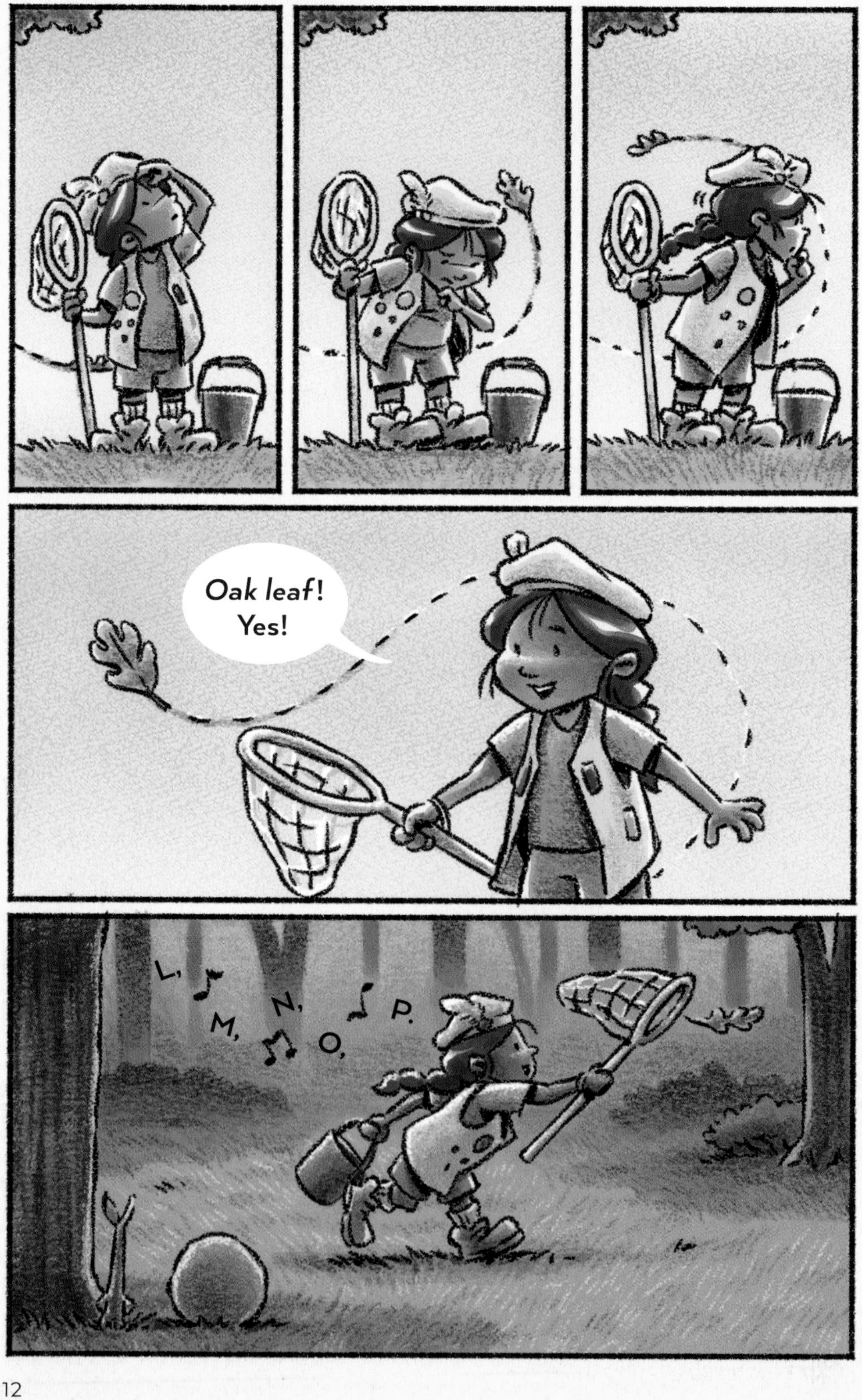
Oak leaf! Yes!
L, M, N, O, P.

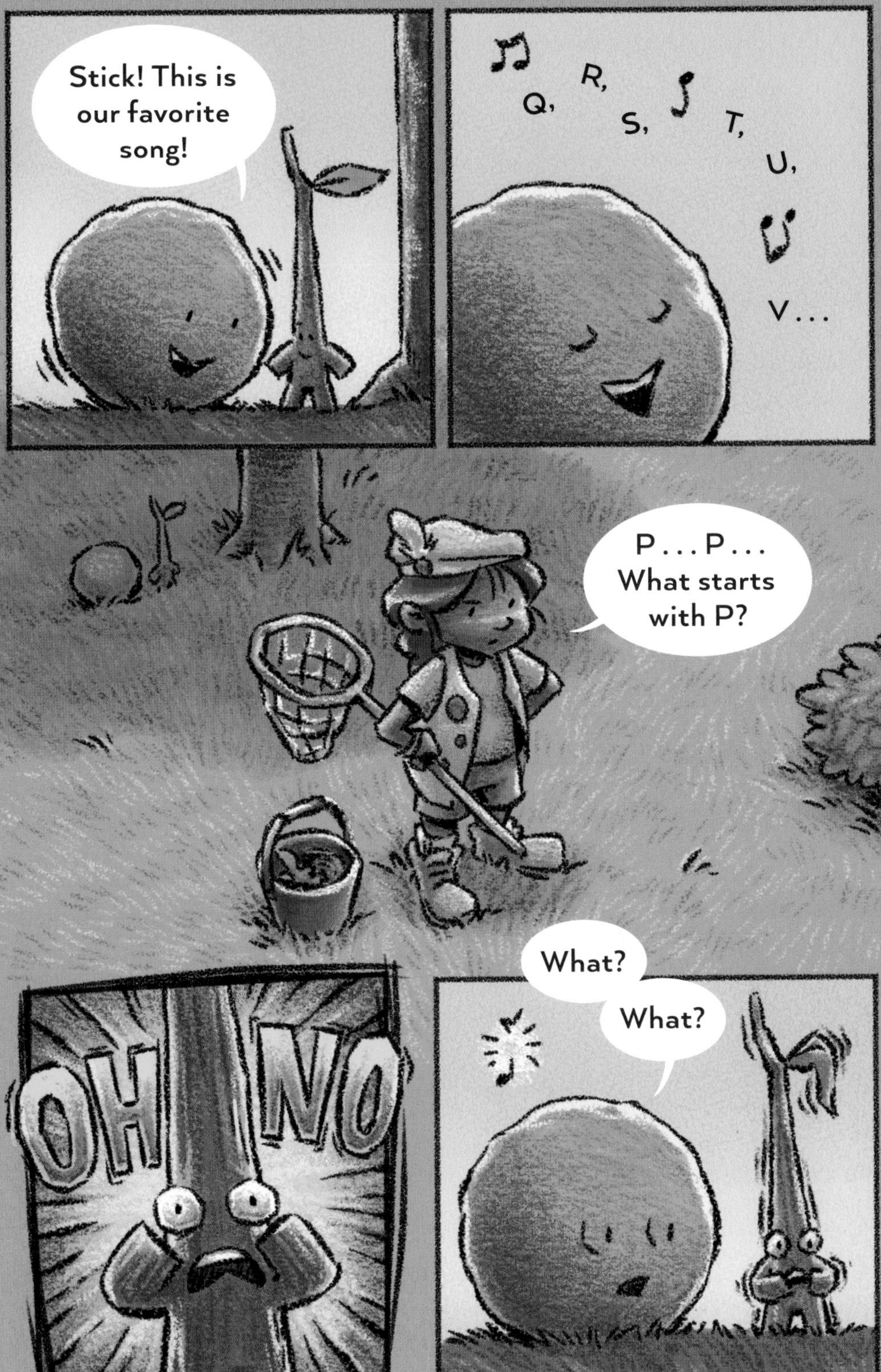
Stick! This is our favorite song!
Q, R, S, T, U, V...
P...P... What starts with P?
OH NO
What?
What?

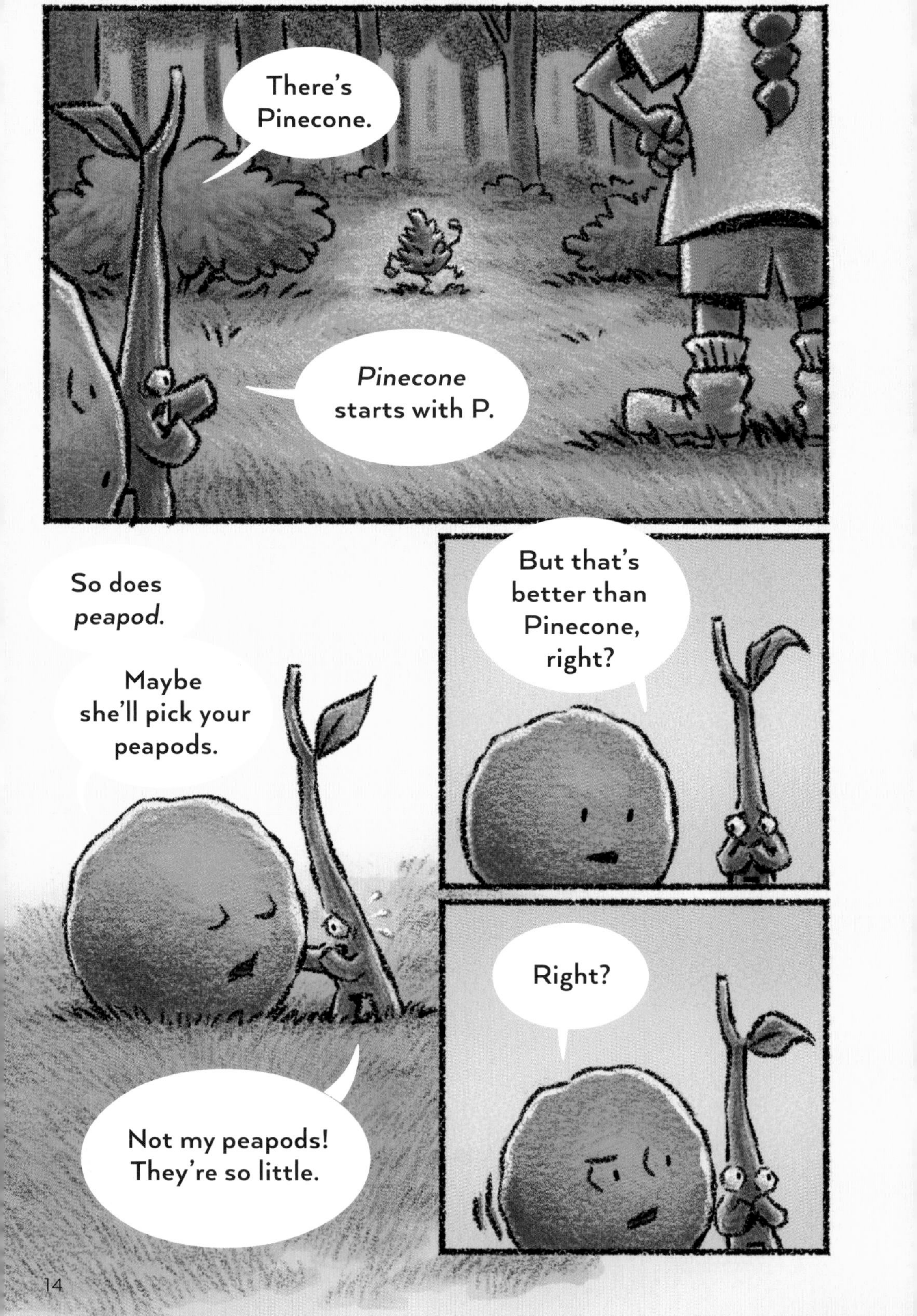
There's Pinecone.
Pinecone starts with P.
So does *peapod*.
Maybe she'll pick your peapods.
Not my peapods! They're so little.
But that's better than Pinecone, right?
Right?

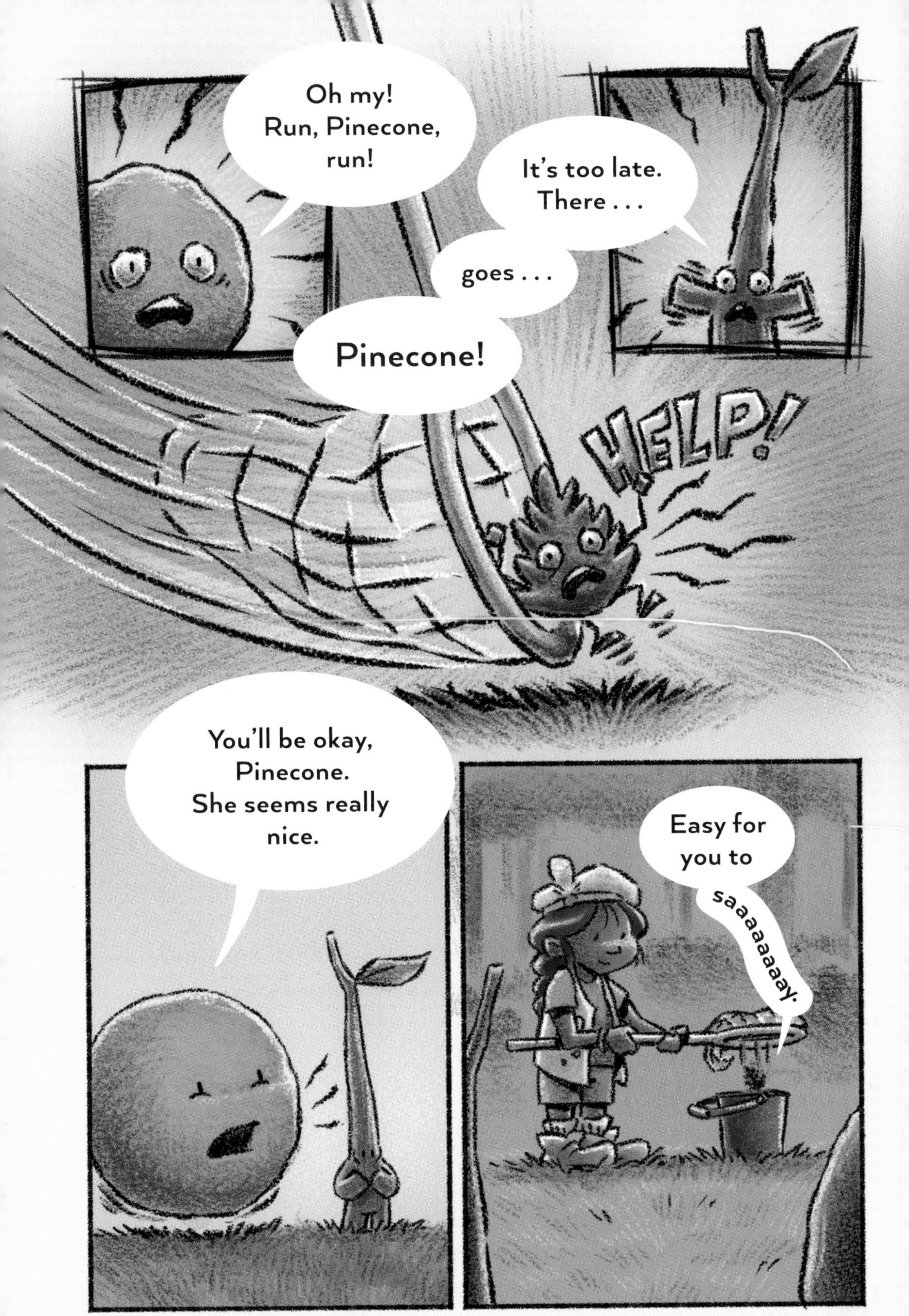
Oh my!
Run, Pinecone,
run!
It's too late.
There . . .
goes . . .
Pinecone!
HELP!
You'll be okay,
Pinecone.
She seems really
nice.
Easy for
you to
saaaaaaaay.

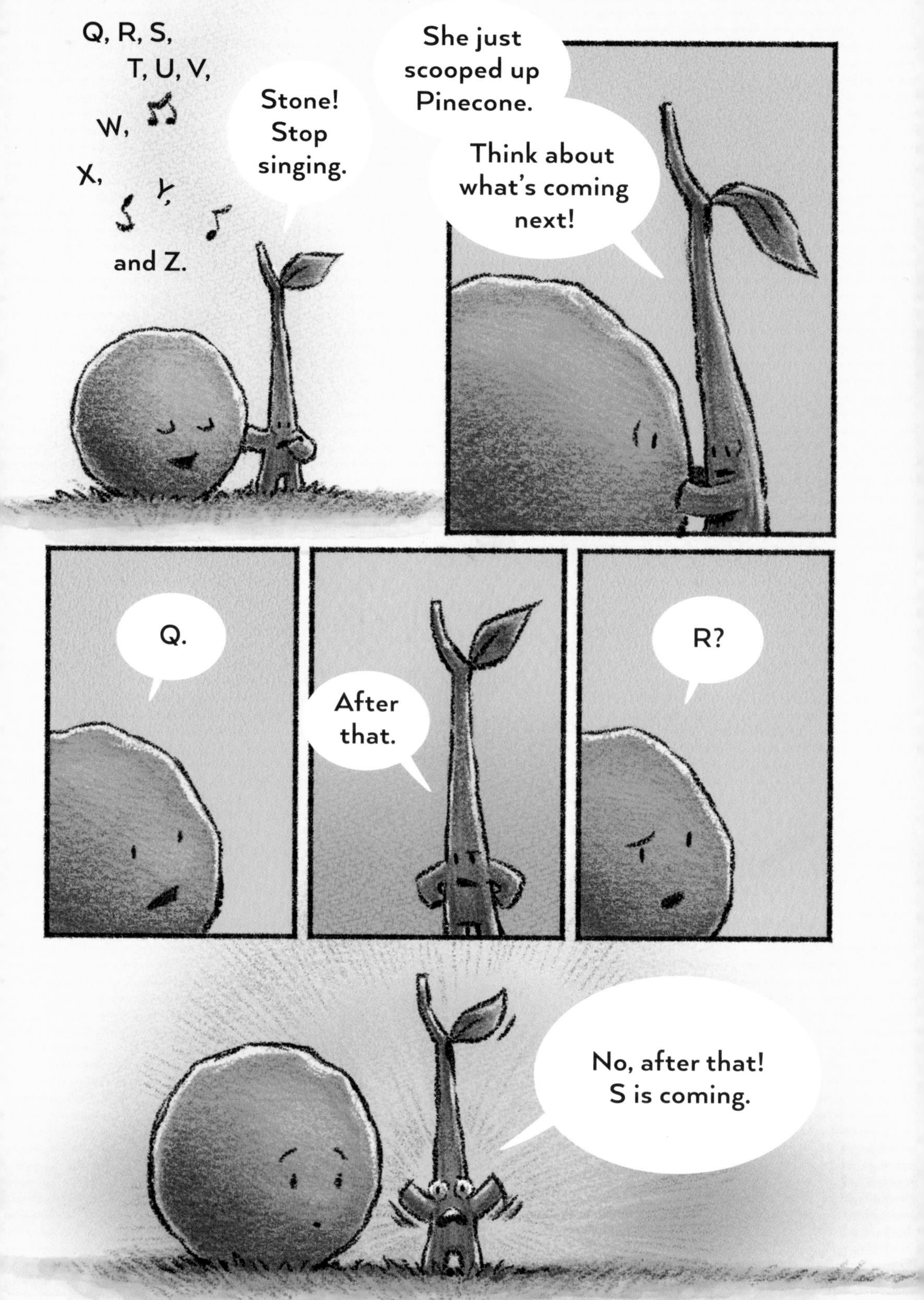
Q, R, S, T, U, V, W, X, Y, and Z.
Stone! Stop singing.
She just scooped up Pinecone.
Think about what's coming next!
Q.
After that.
R?
No, after that! S is coming.

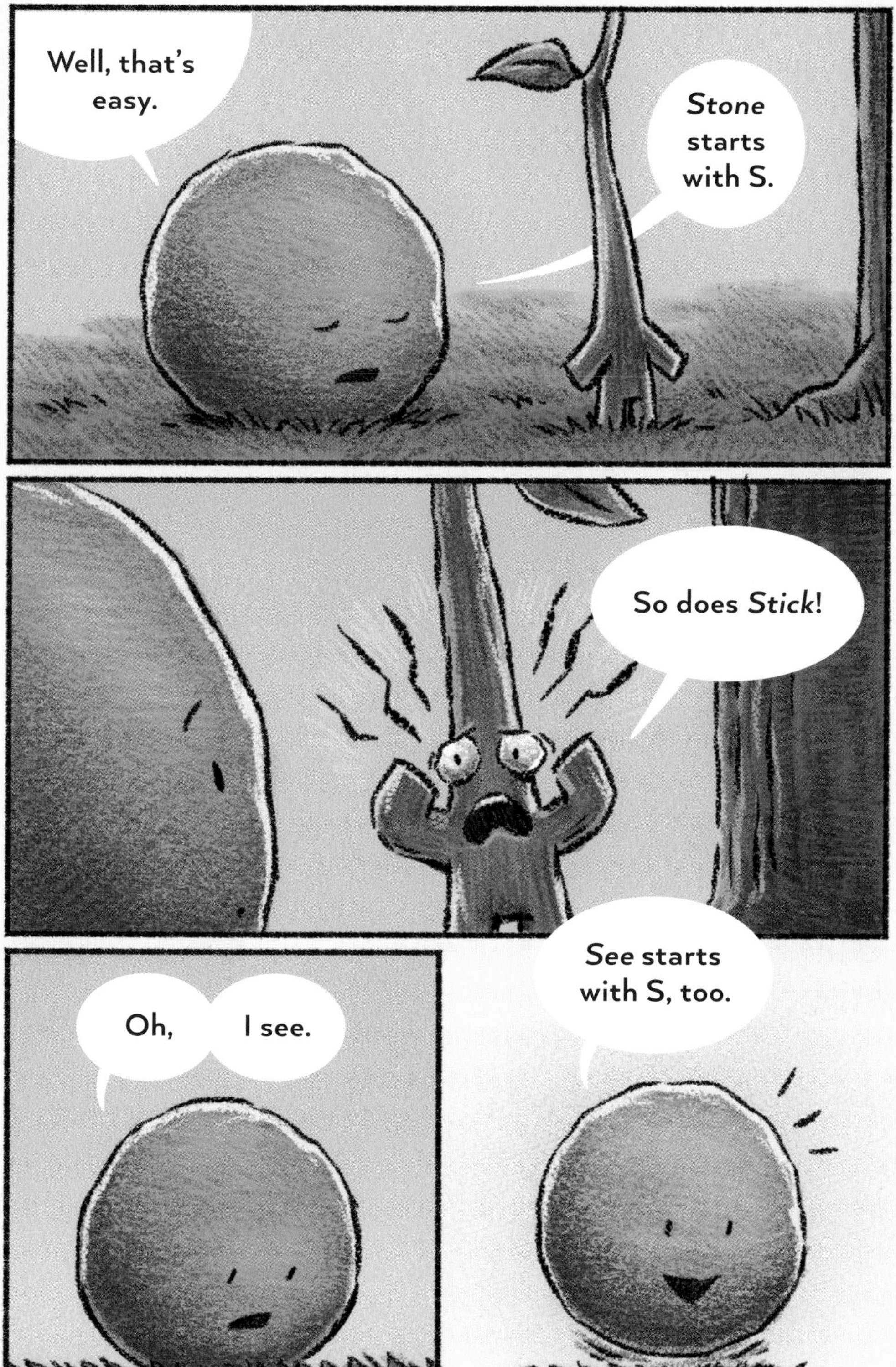
Well, that's easy.
Stone starts with S.
So does *Stick*!
Oh,
I see.
See starts with S, too.

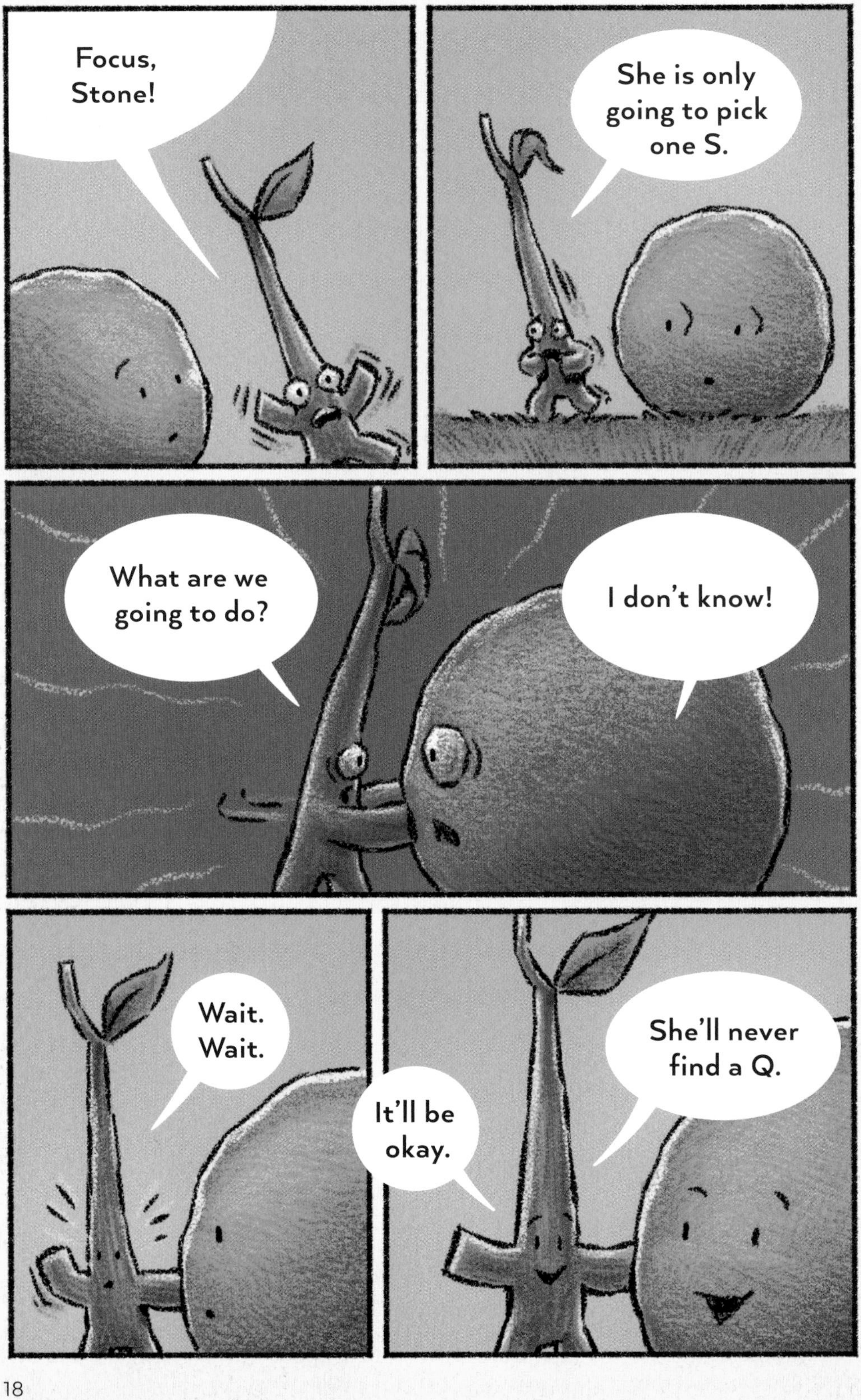

Focus, Stone!
She is only going to pick one S.
What are we going to do?
I don't know!
Wait. Wait.
It'll be okay.
She'll never find a Q.

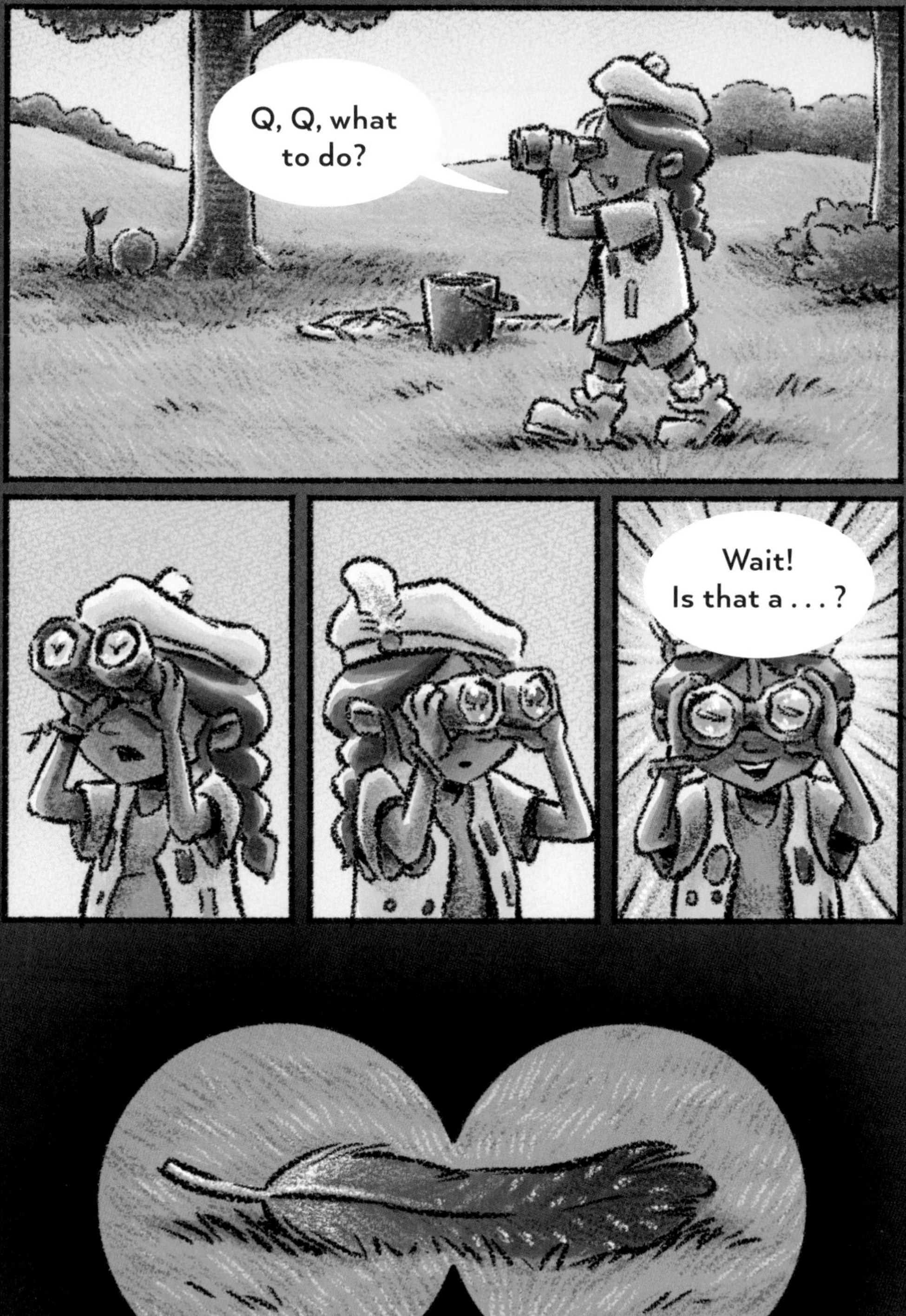
Q, Q, what to do?
Wait! Is that a . . . ?

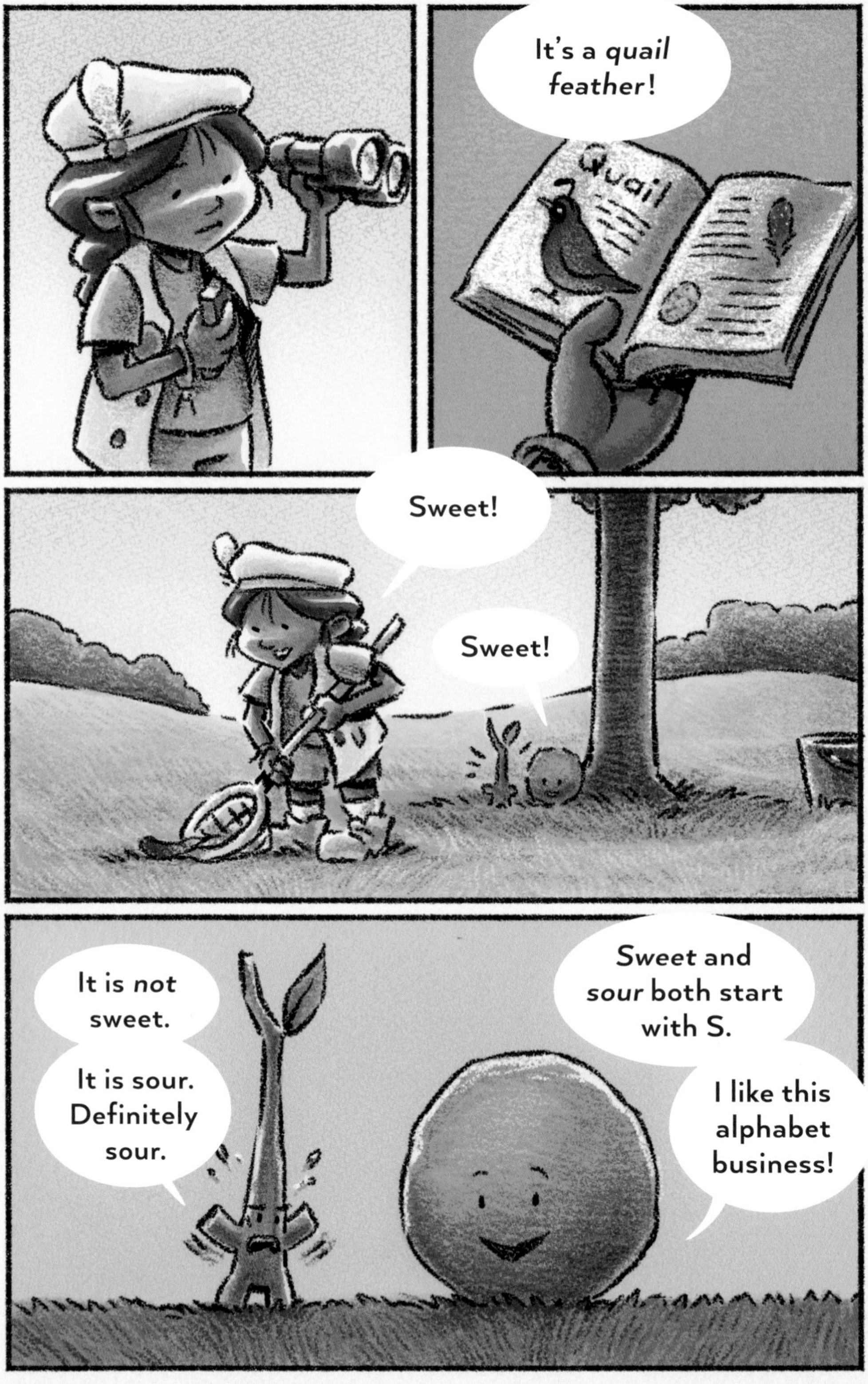
It's a *quail* *feather*!
Quail
Sweet!
Sweet!
It is *not* sweet.
It is sour. Definitely sour.
Sweet and *sour* both start with S.
I like this alphabet business!

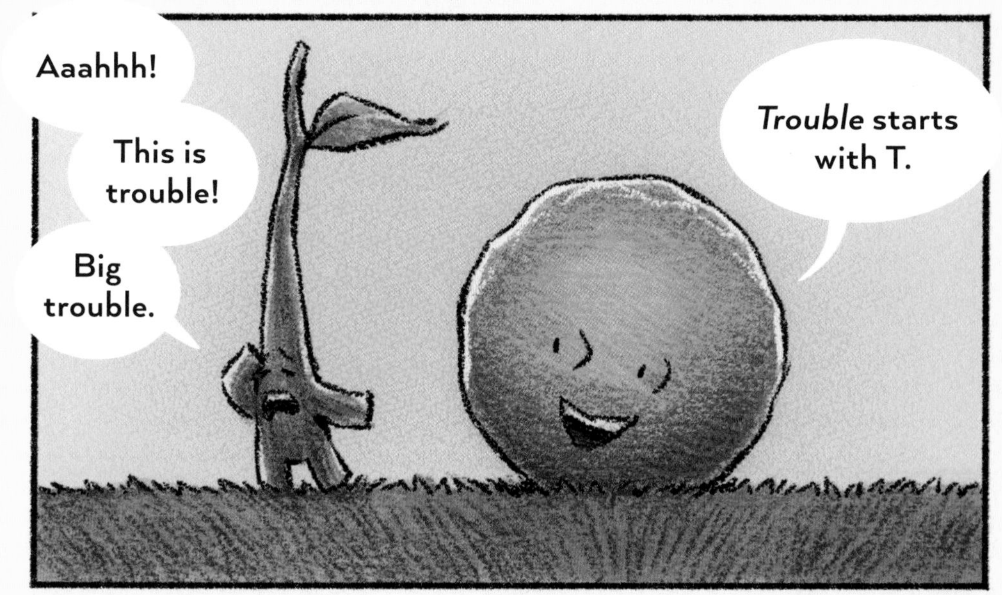
Aaahhh!
This is trouble!
Big trouble.
Trouble starts with T.

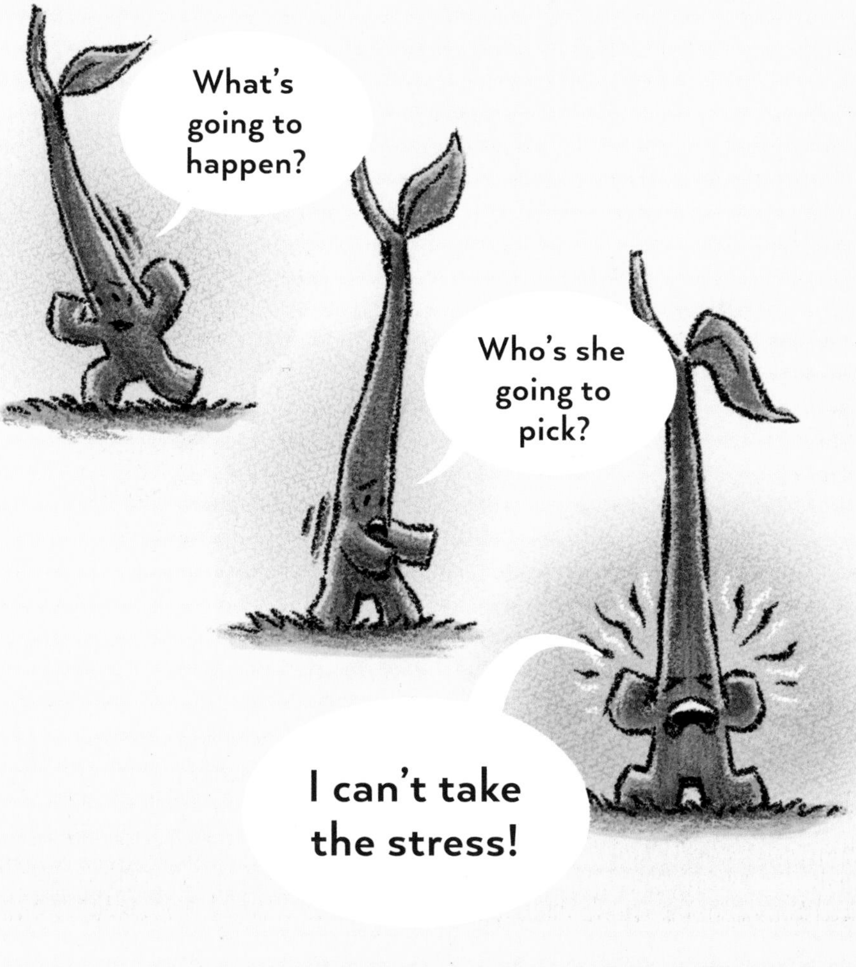
What's going to happen?
Who's she going to pick?
I can't take the stress!

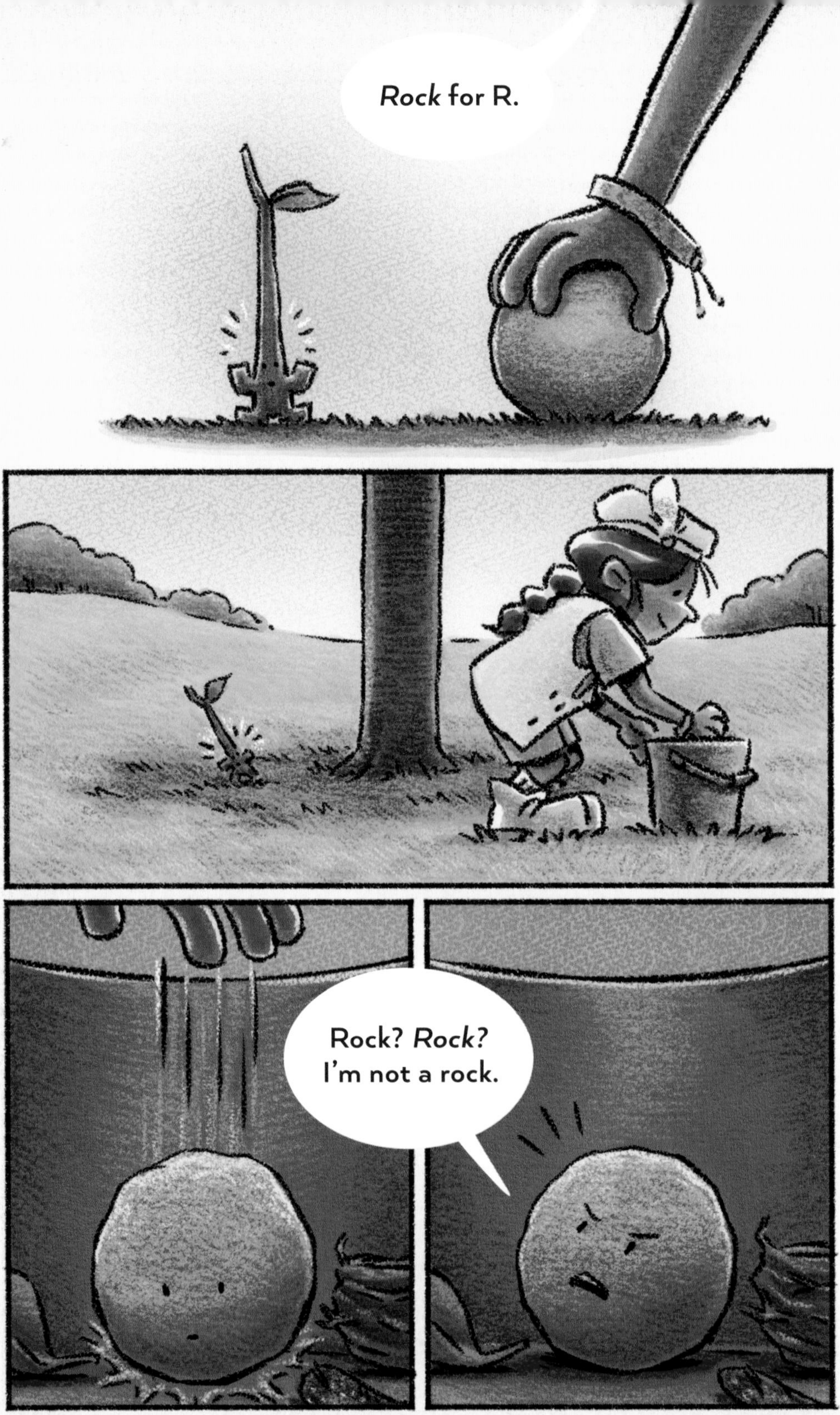

Rock for R.
Rock? *Rock?* I'm not a rock.

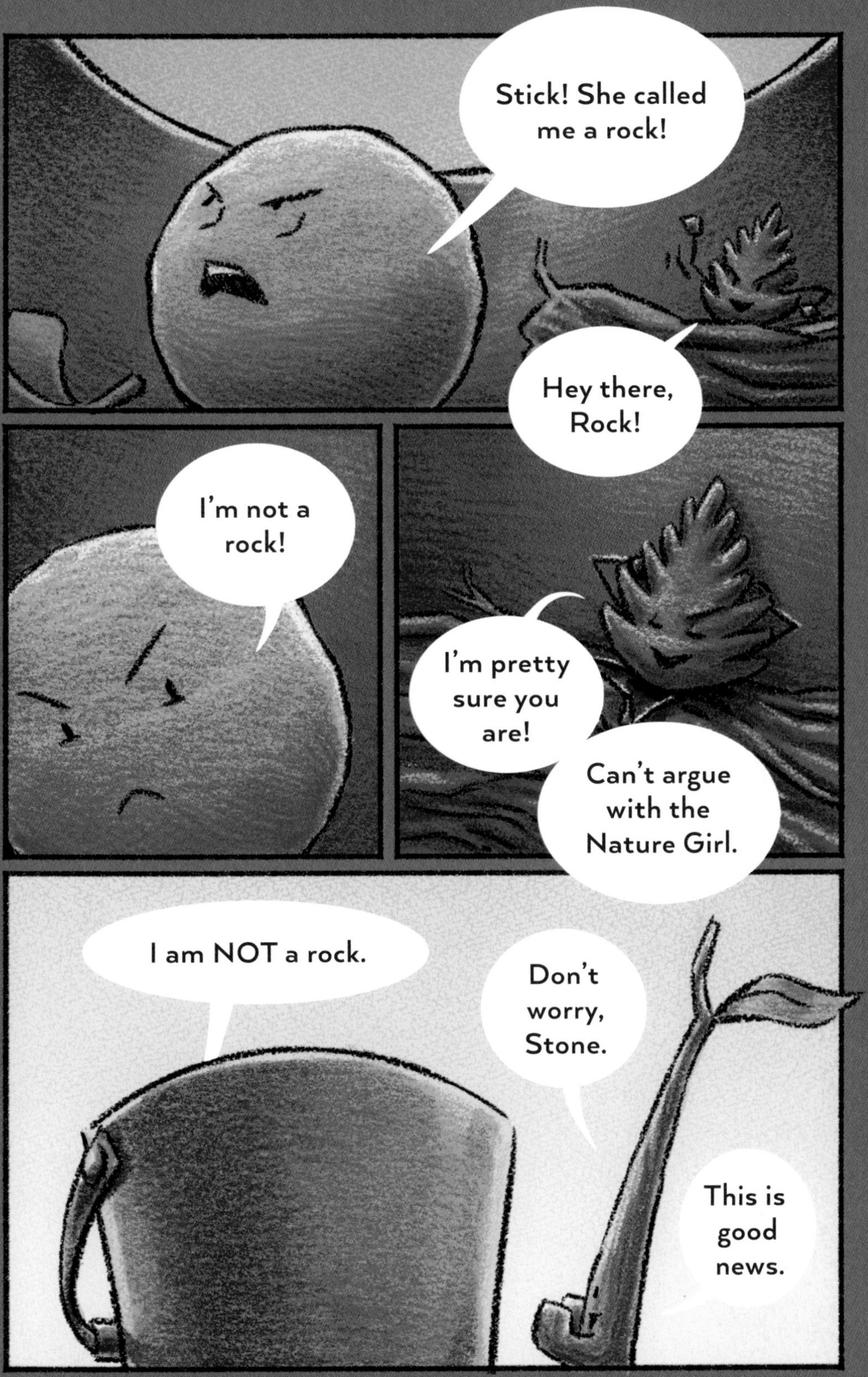
Stick! She called me a rock!
Hey there, Rock!
I'm not a rock!
I'm pretty sure you are!
Can't argue with the Nature Girl.
I am NOT a rock.
Don't worry, Stone.
This is good news.

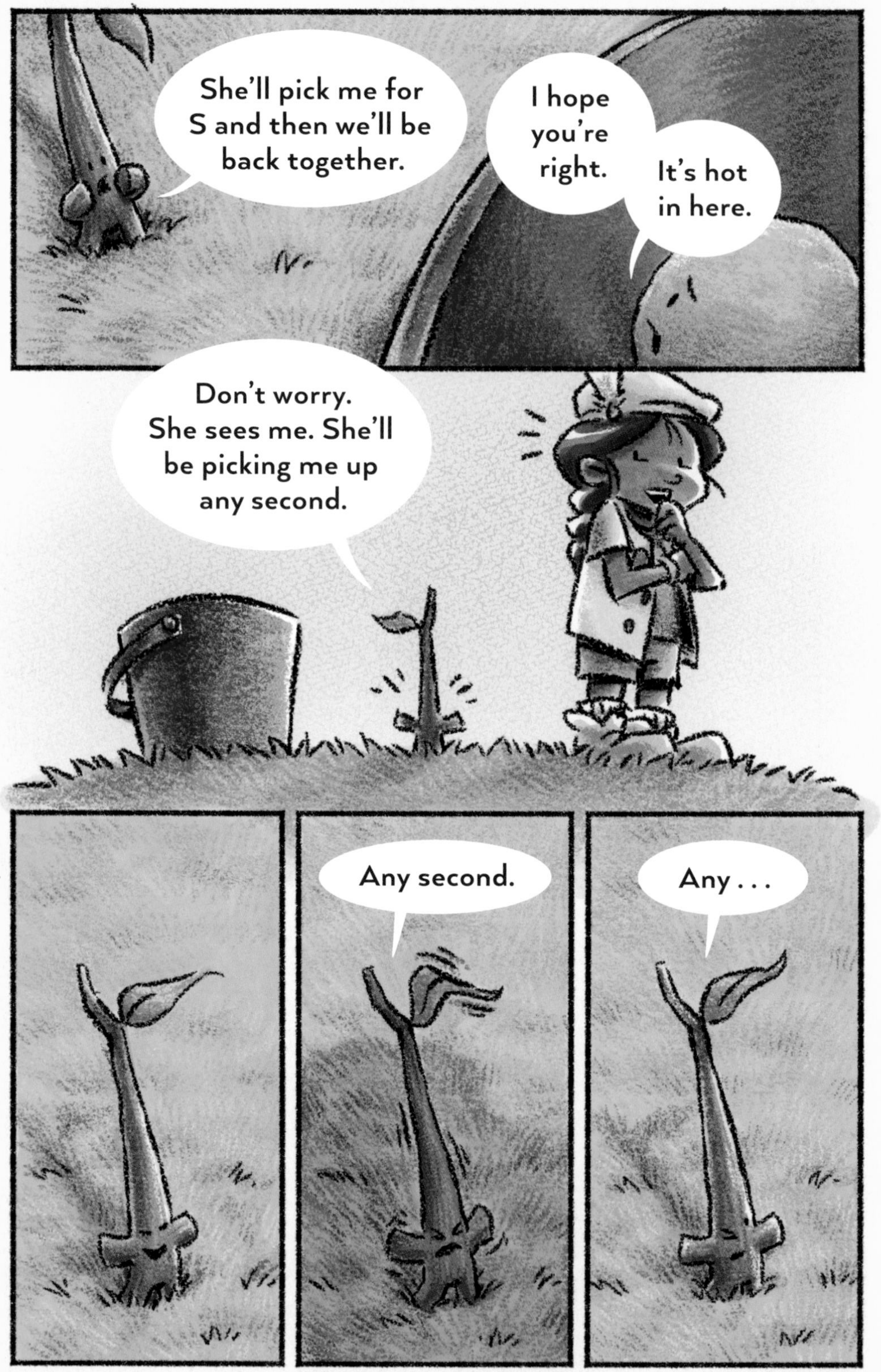
She'll pick me for S and then we'll be back together.
I hope you're right.
It's hot in here.
Don't worry. She sees me. She'll be picking me up any second.
Any second.
Any . . .

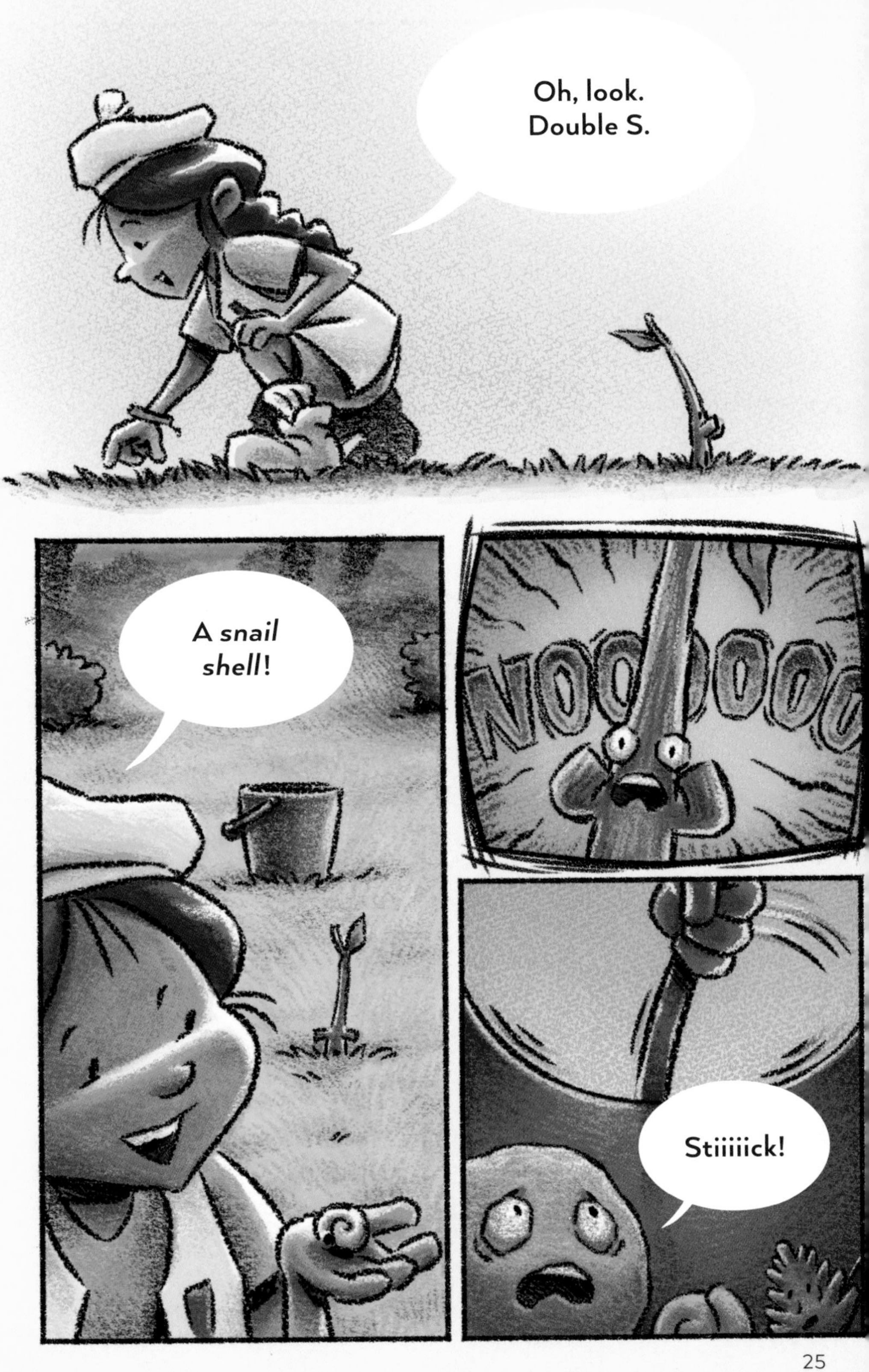
Oh, look.
Double S.
A *snail shell*!
NOOOOOO
Stiiiiick!

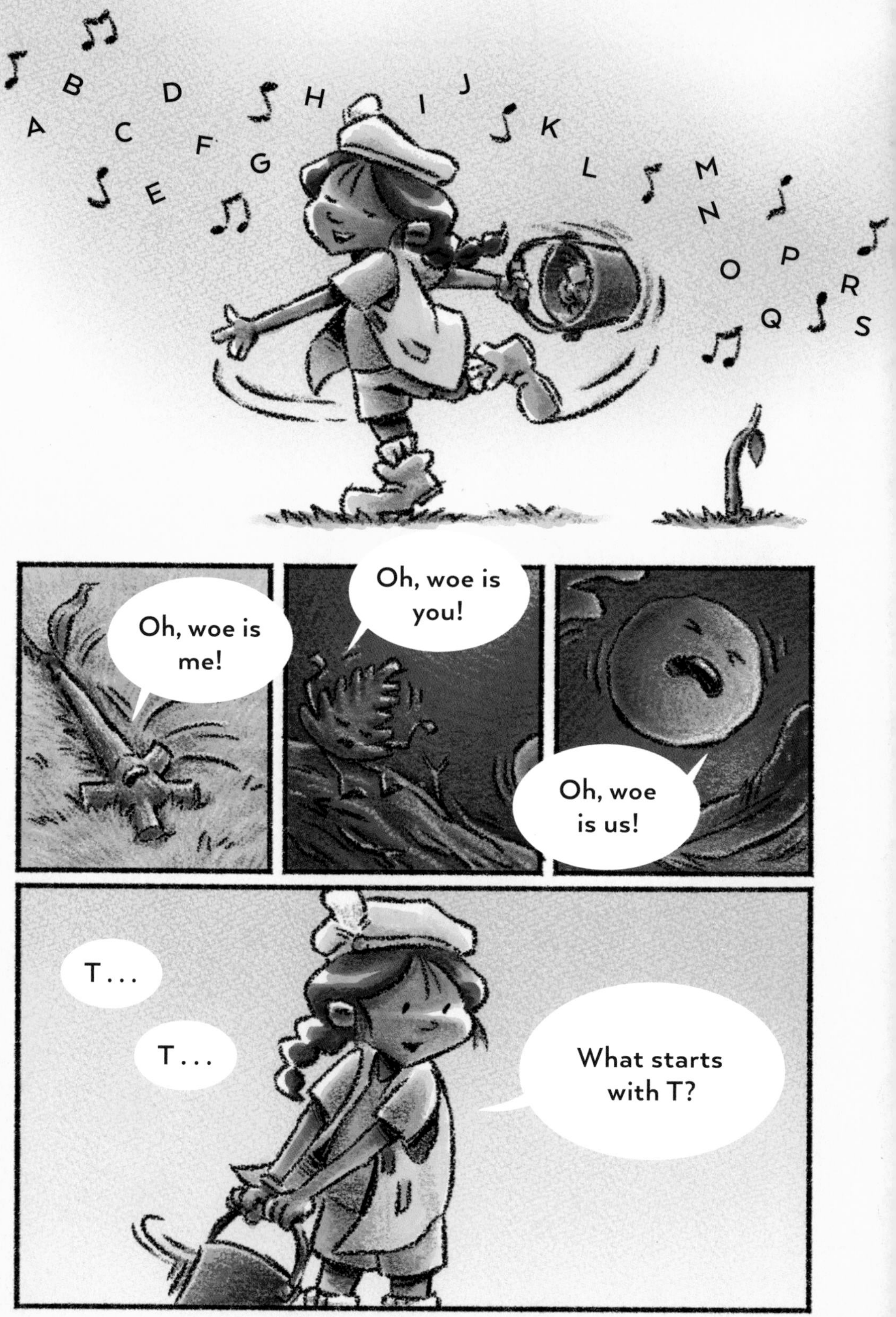
A B C D E F G H I J K L M N O P Q R S
Oh, woe is me!
Oh, woe is you!
Oh, woe is us!
T . . .
T . . .
What starts with T?

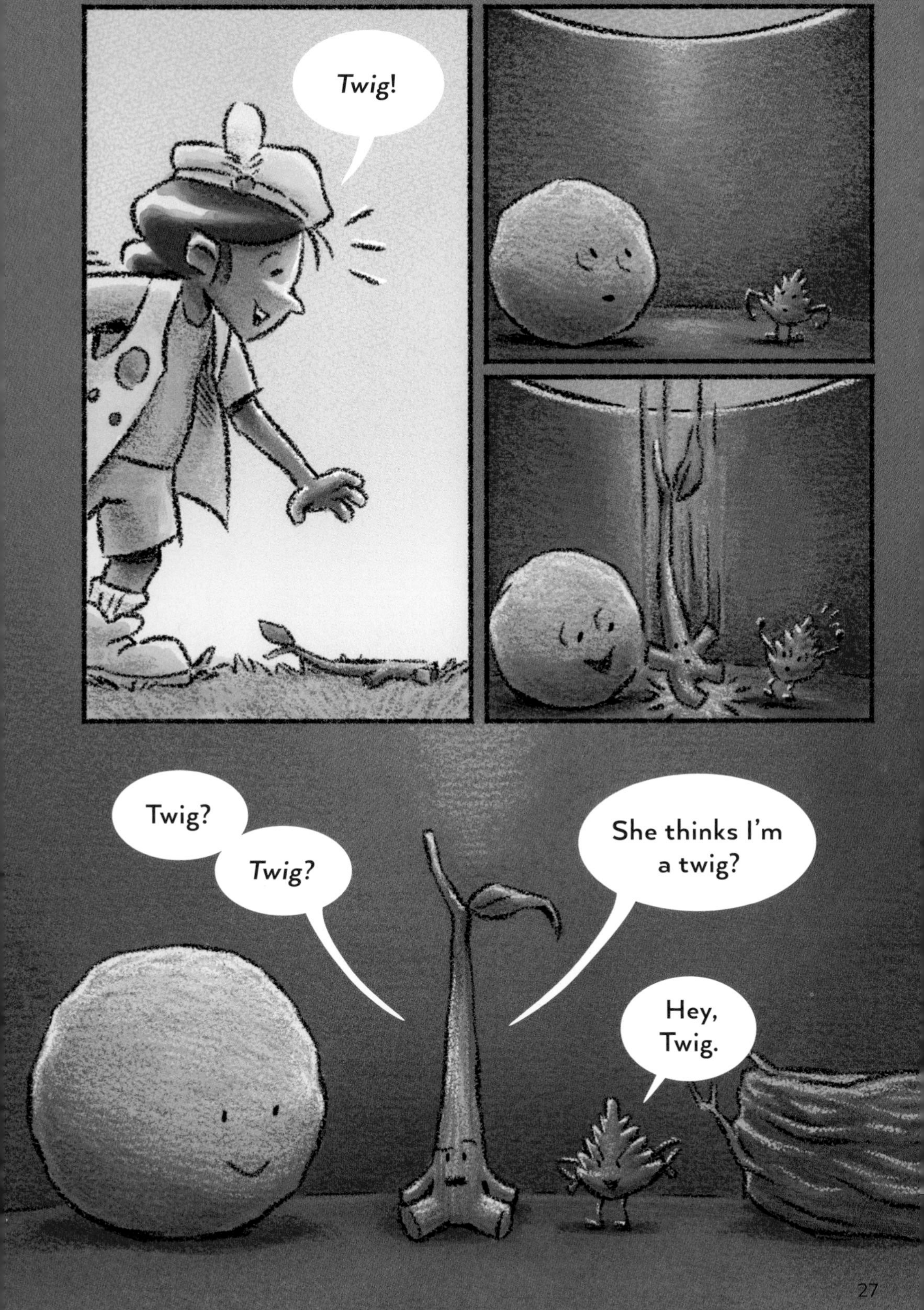
Twig!
Twig?
Twig?
She thinks I'm a twig?
Hey, Twig.

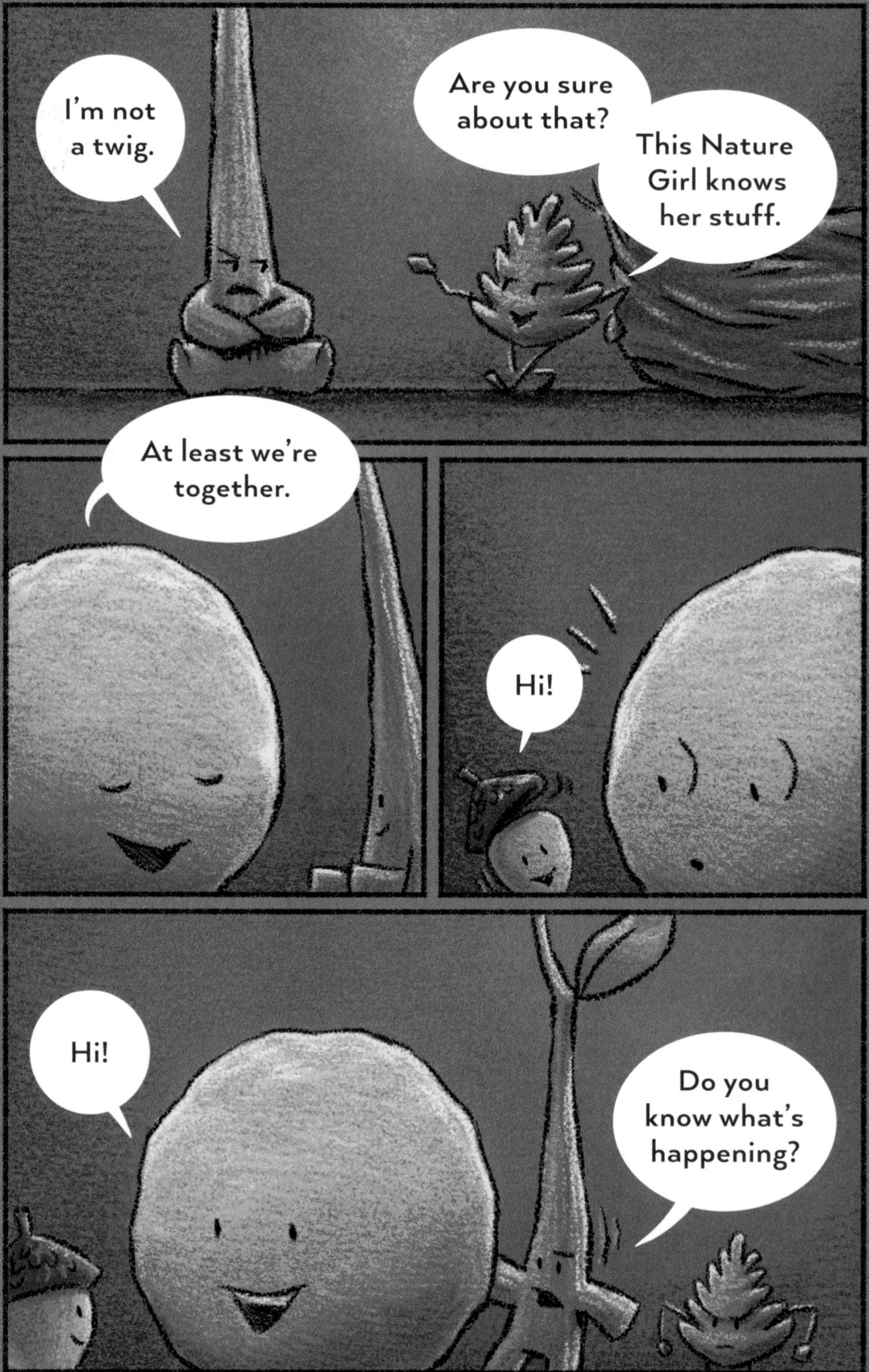
I'm not a twig.
Are you sure about that?
This Nature Girl knows her stuff.
At least we're together.
Hi!
Hi!
Do you know what's happening?

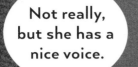

Not really, but she has a nice voice.

Do you know where we're going?

No, but I made some new friends. Say hi to Beetle and Corn.

We've been here all day.

I'm so hot, I could pop!

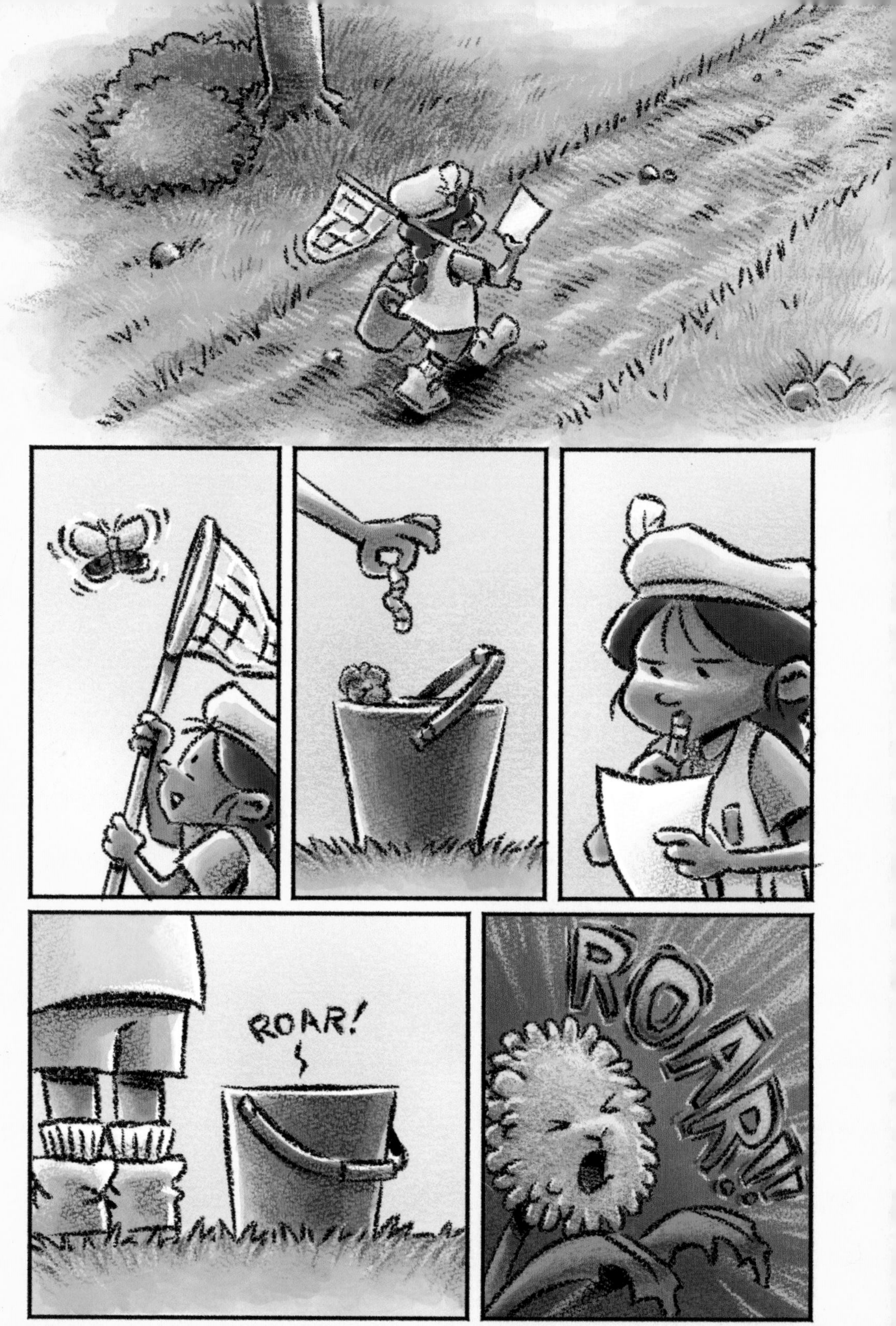
ROAR!
ROAR!!

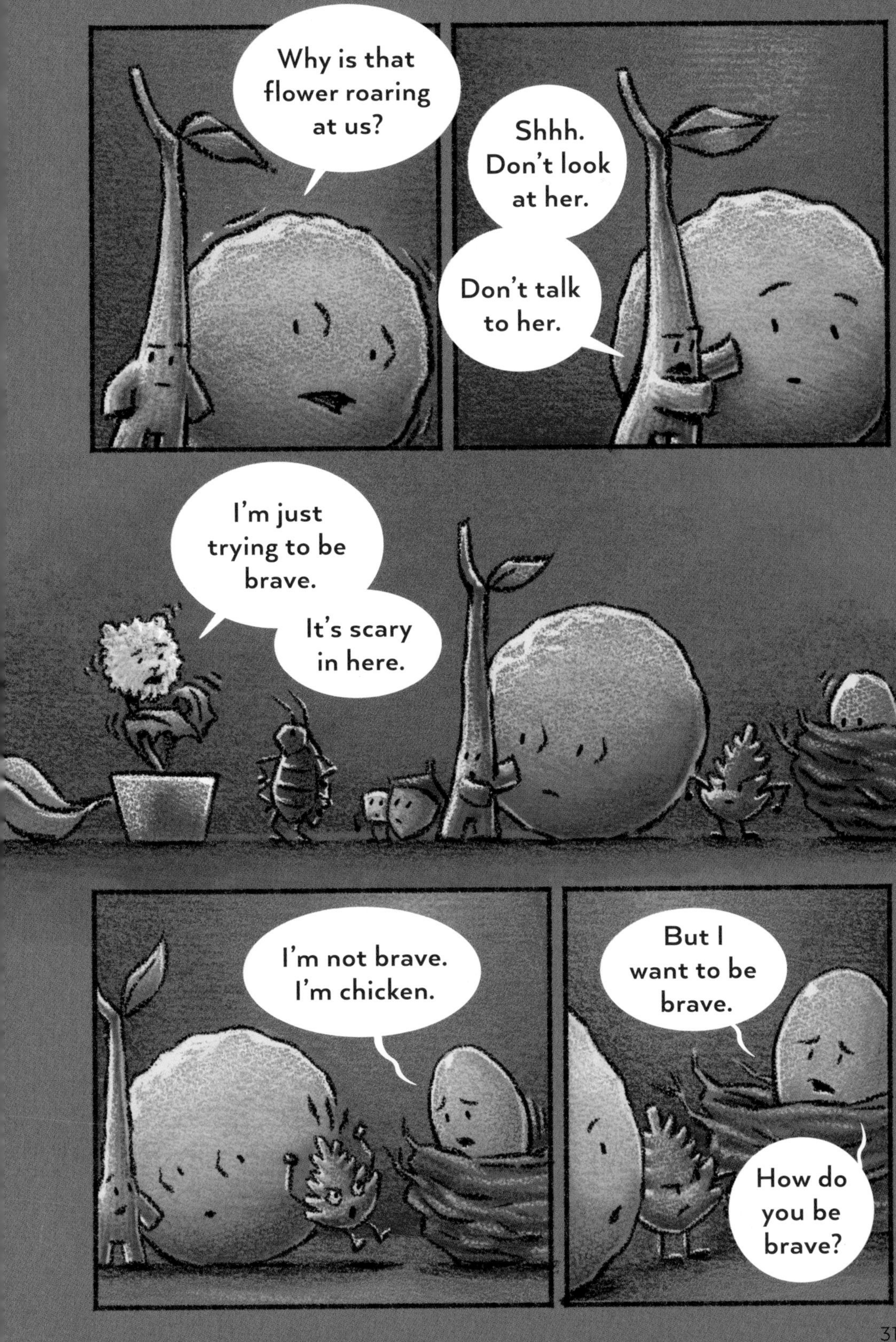
Why is that flower roaring at us?
Shhh. Don't look at her.
Don't talk to her.
I'm just trying to be brave.
It's scary in here.
I'm not brave. I'm chicken.
But I want to be brave.
How do you be brave?

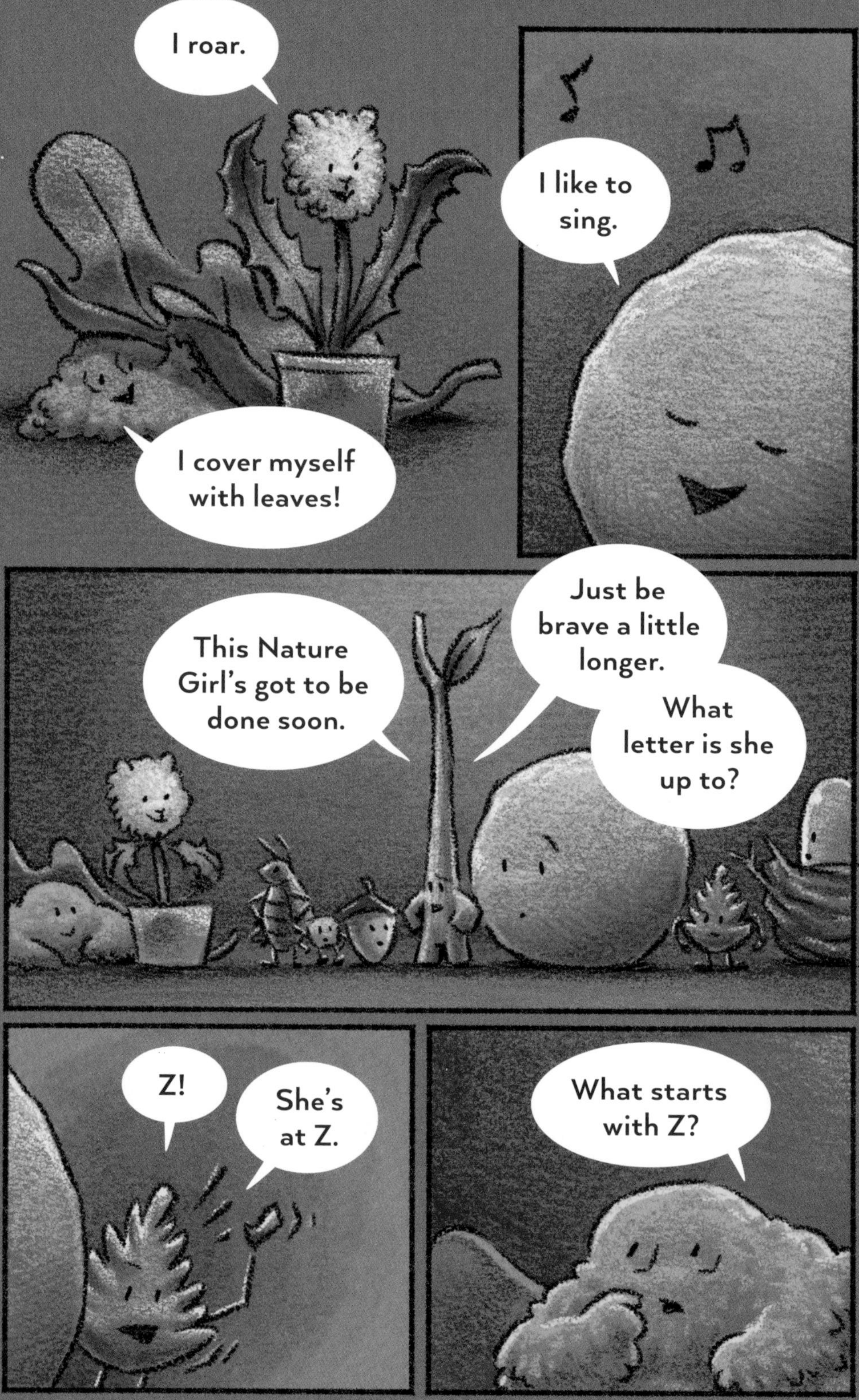
I roar.
I cover myself with leaves!
I like to sing.
This Nature Girl's got to be done soon.
Just be brave a little longer.
What letter is she up to?
Z!
She's at Z.
What starts with Z?

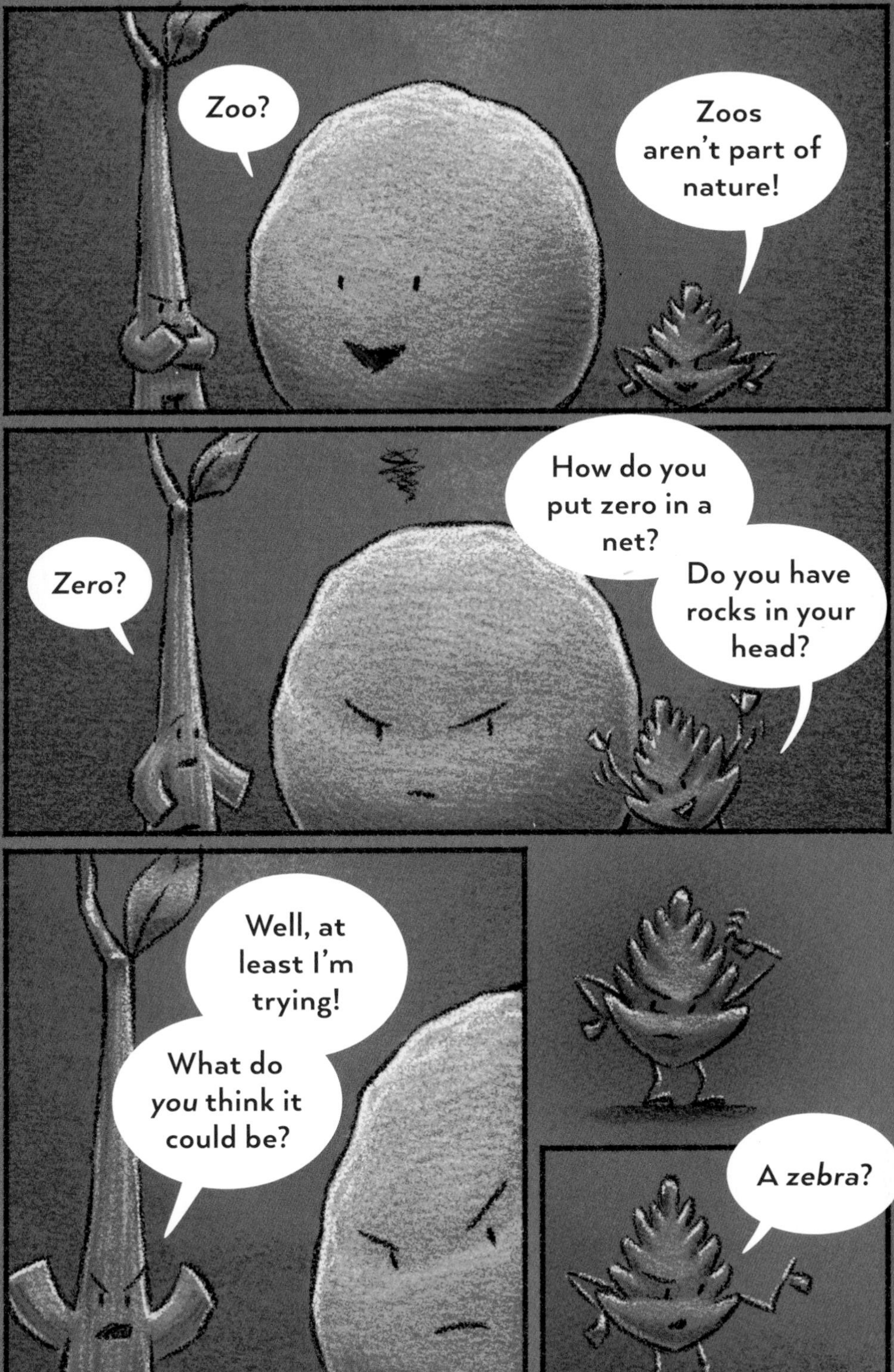
Zoo?
Zoos aren't part of nature!
Zero?
How do you put zero in a net?
Do you have rocks in your head?
Well, at least I'm trying!
What do *you* think it could be?
A *zebra*?

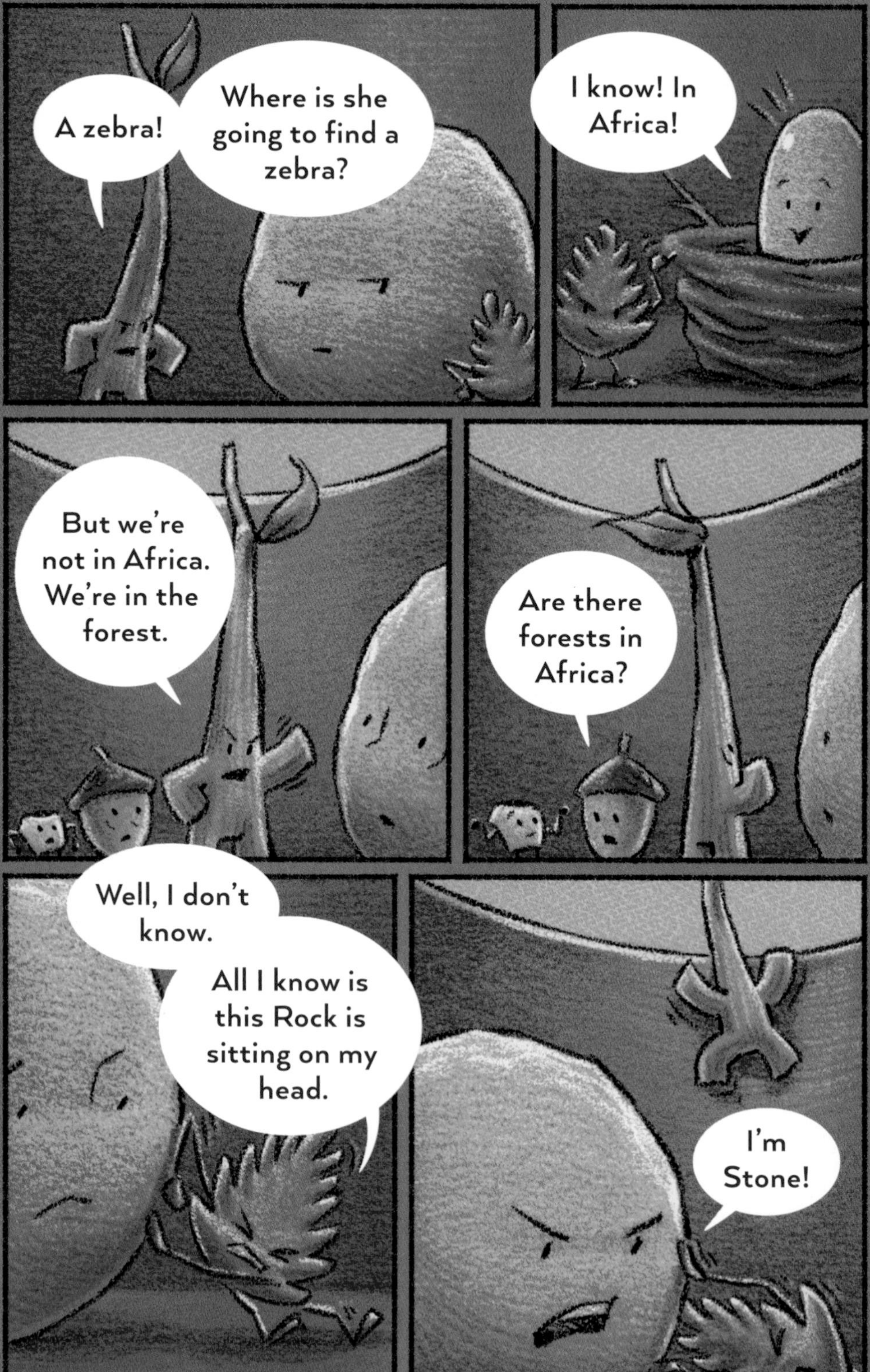
A zebra!
Where is she going to find a zebra?
I know! In Africa!
But we're not in Africa. We're in the forest.
Are there forests in Africa?
Well, I don't know.
All I know is this Rock is sitting on my head.
I'm Stone!

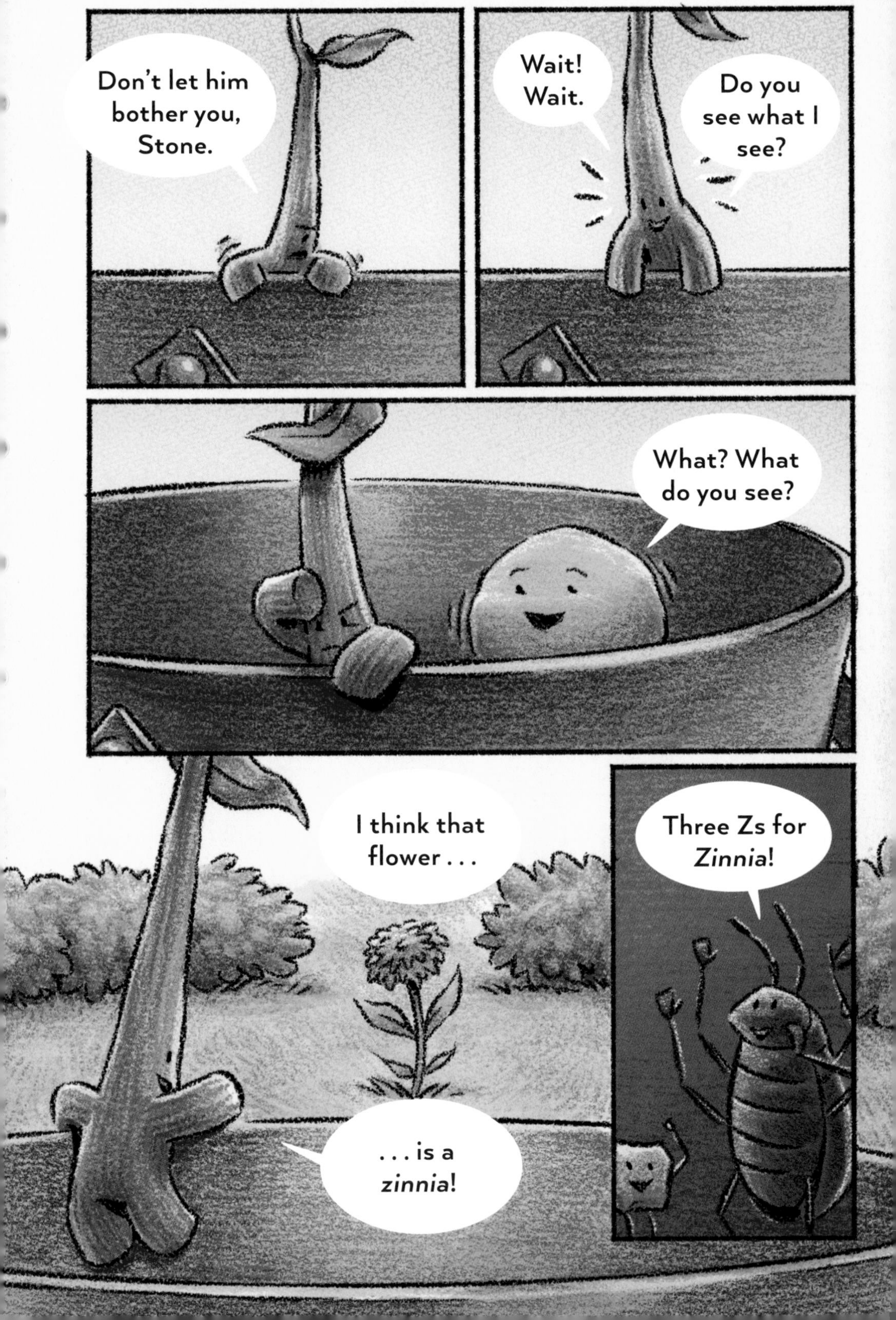
Don't let him bother you, Stone.
Wait! Wait.
Do you see what I see?
What? What do you see?
I think that flower . . .
. . . is a *zinnia*!
Three Zs for *Zinnia*!

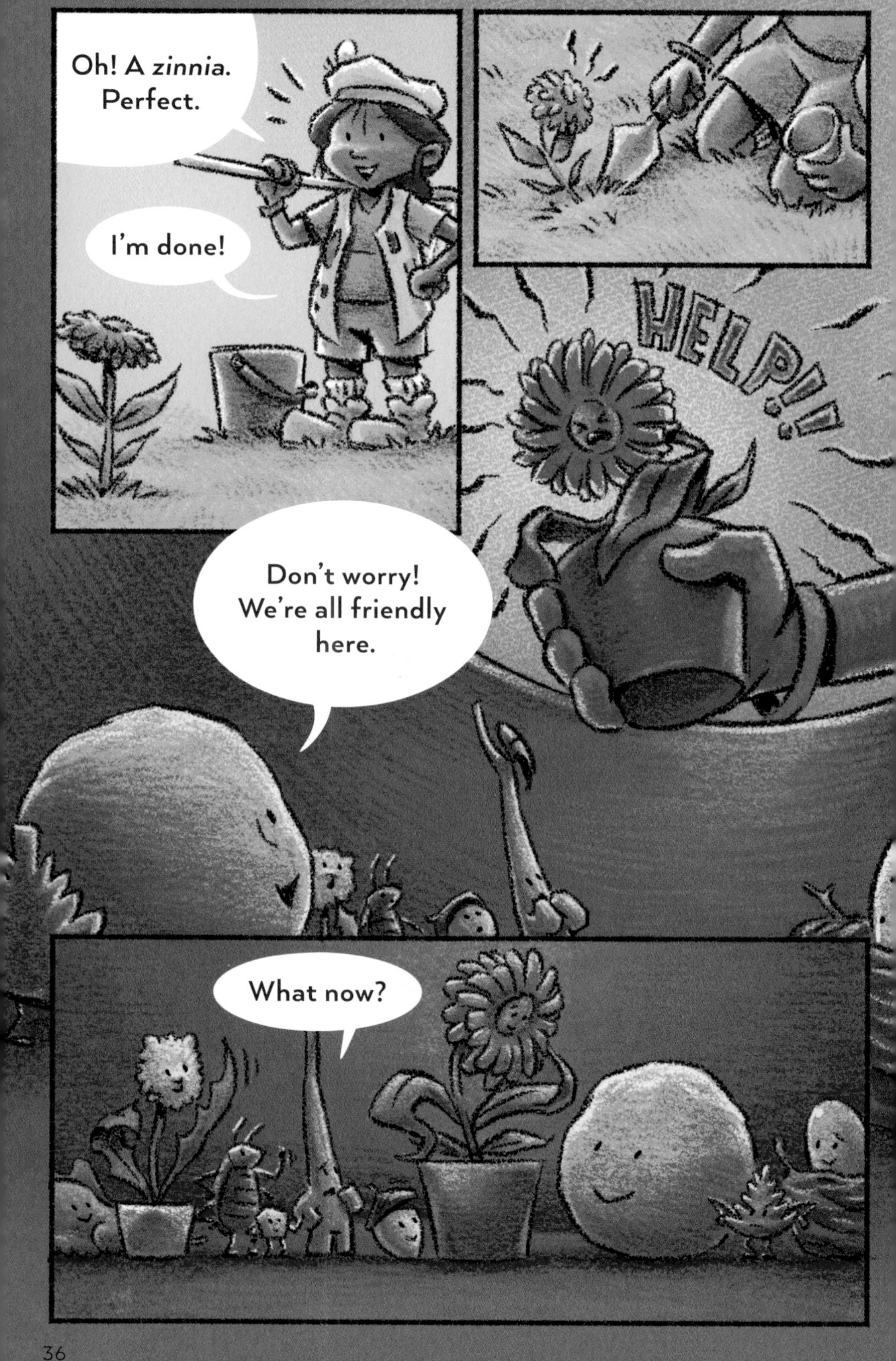
Oh! A *zinnia*. Perfect.
I'm done!
HELP!!!
Don't worry! We're all friendly here.
What now?

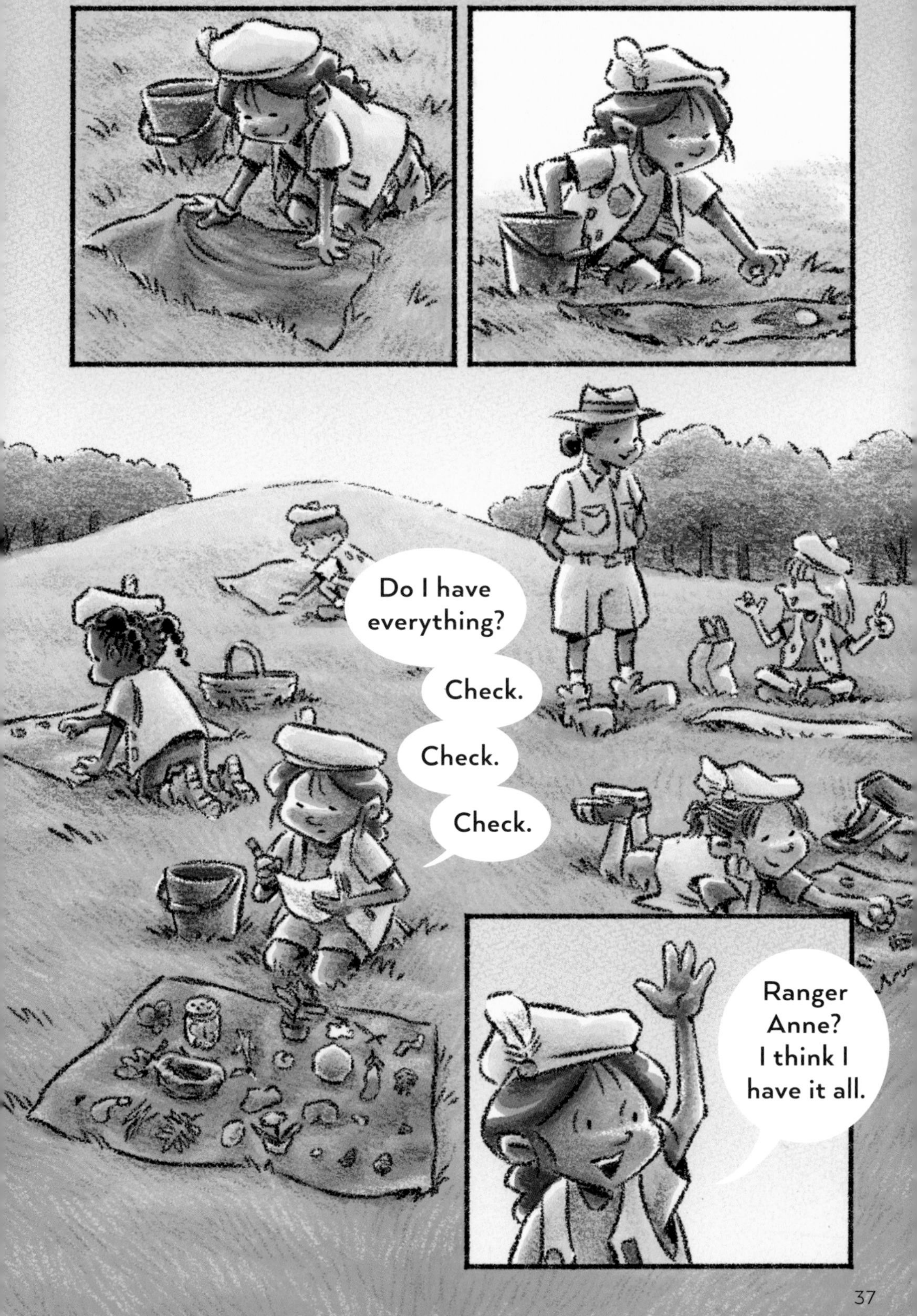
Do I have everything?
Check.
Check.
Check.
Ranger Anne? I think I have it all.

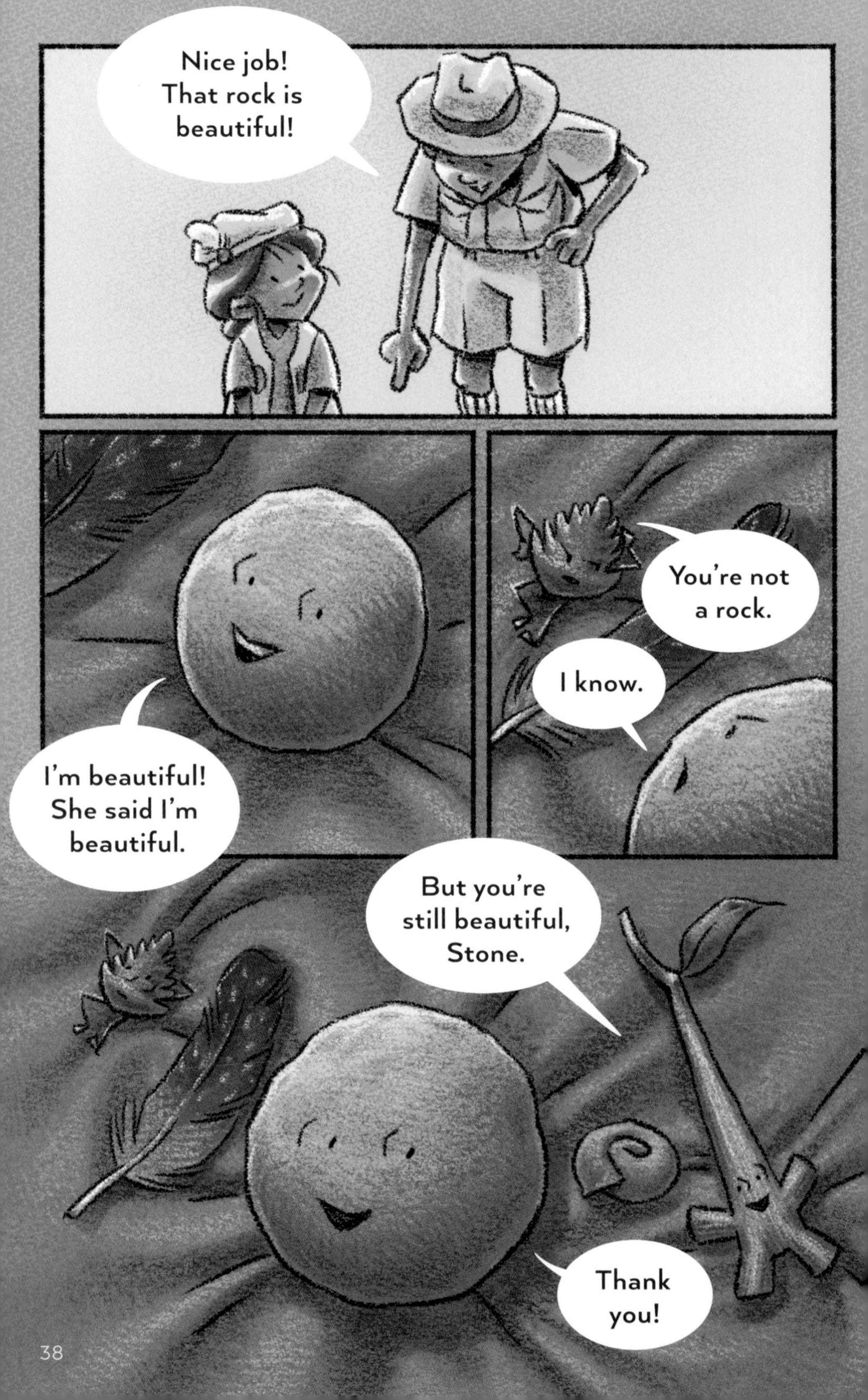
Nice job! That rock is beautiful!
I'm beautiful! She said I'm beautiful.
You're not a rock.
I know.
But you're still beautiful, Stone.
Thank you!

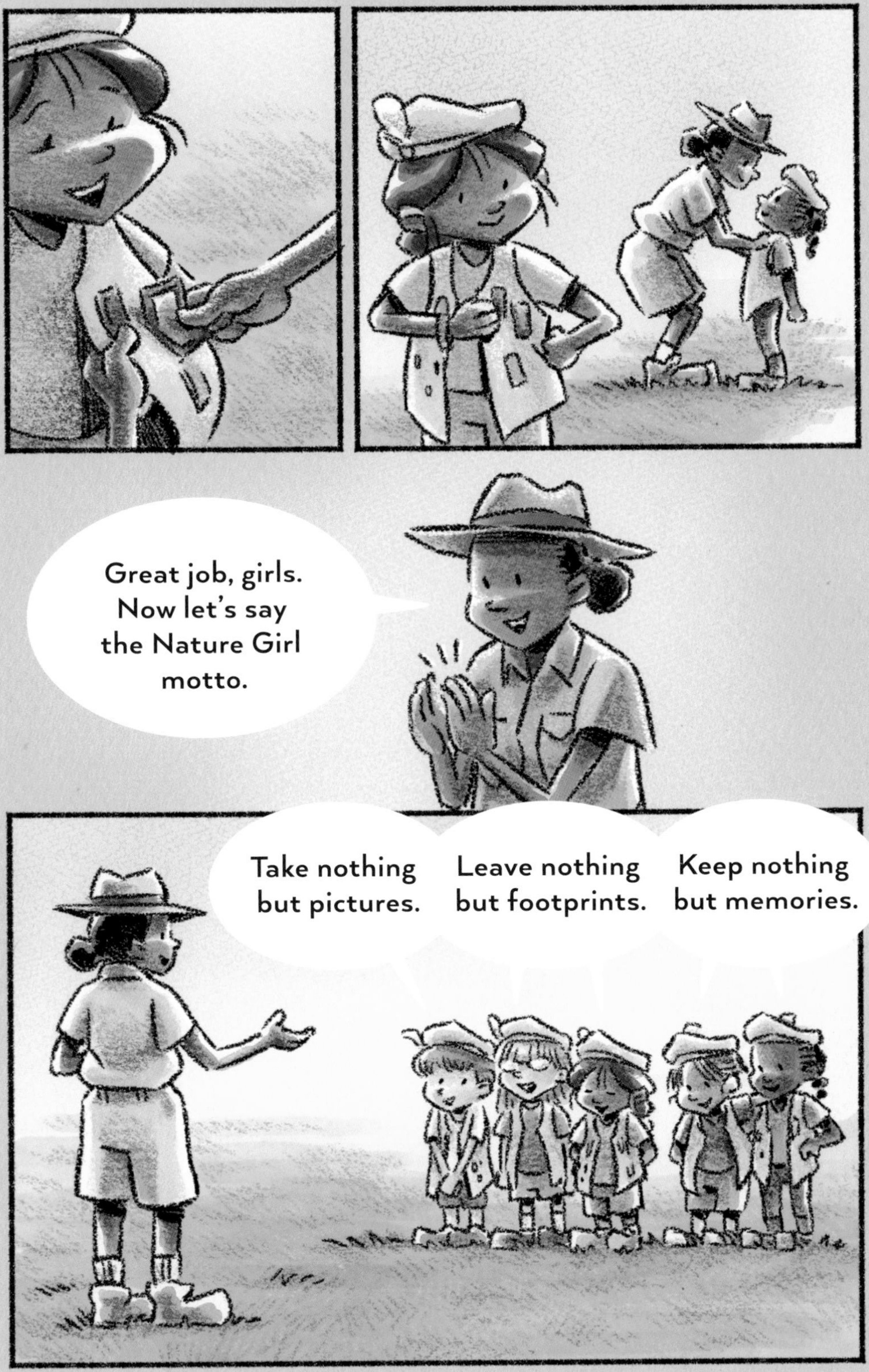
Great job, girls. Now let's say the Nature Girl motto.
Take nothing but pictures.
Leave nothing but footprints.
Keep nothing but memories.

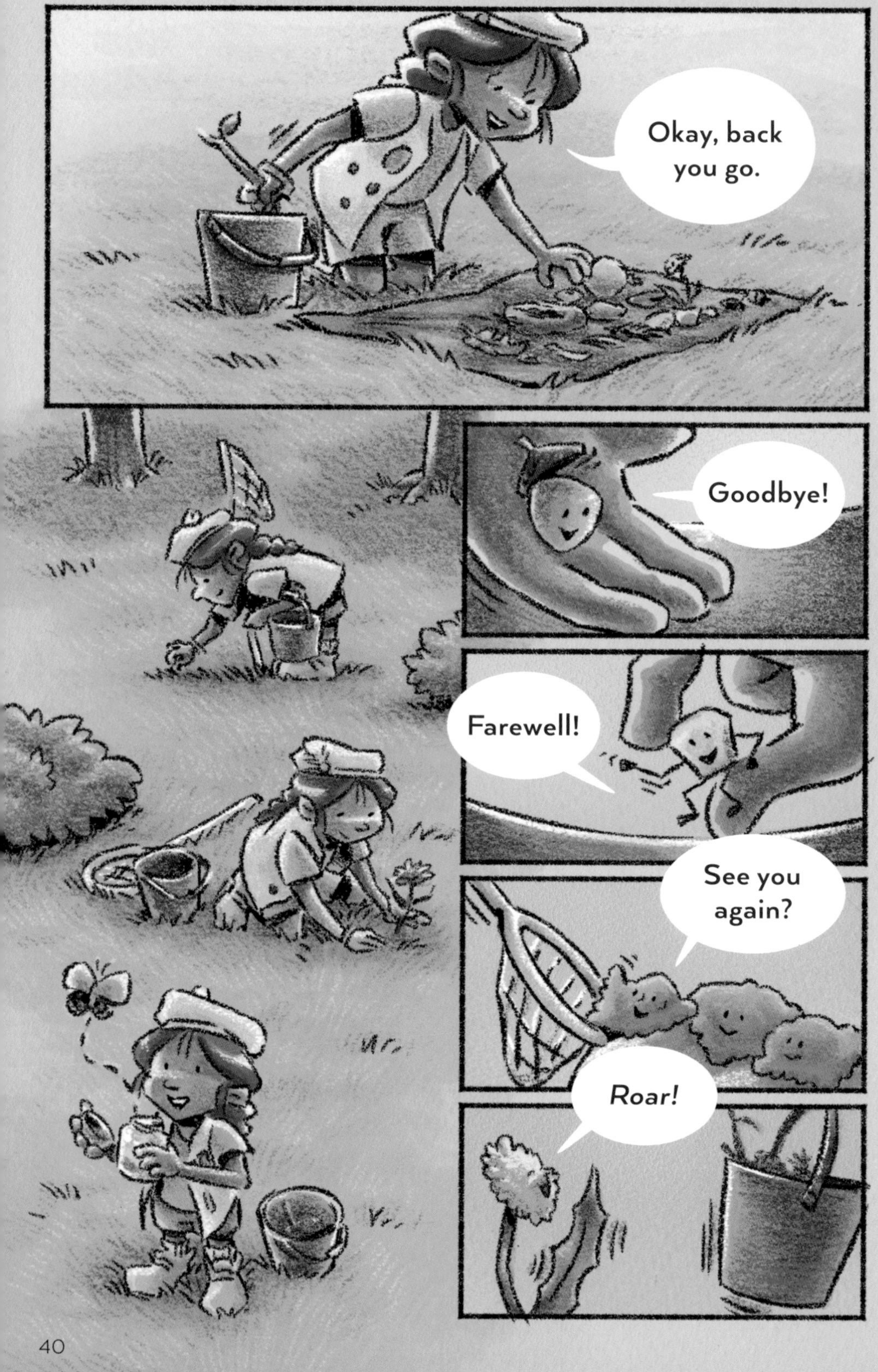
Okay, back you go.
Goodbye!
Farewell!
See you again?
Roar!

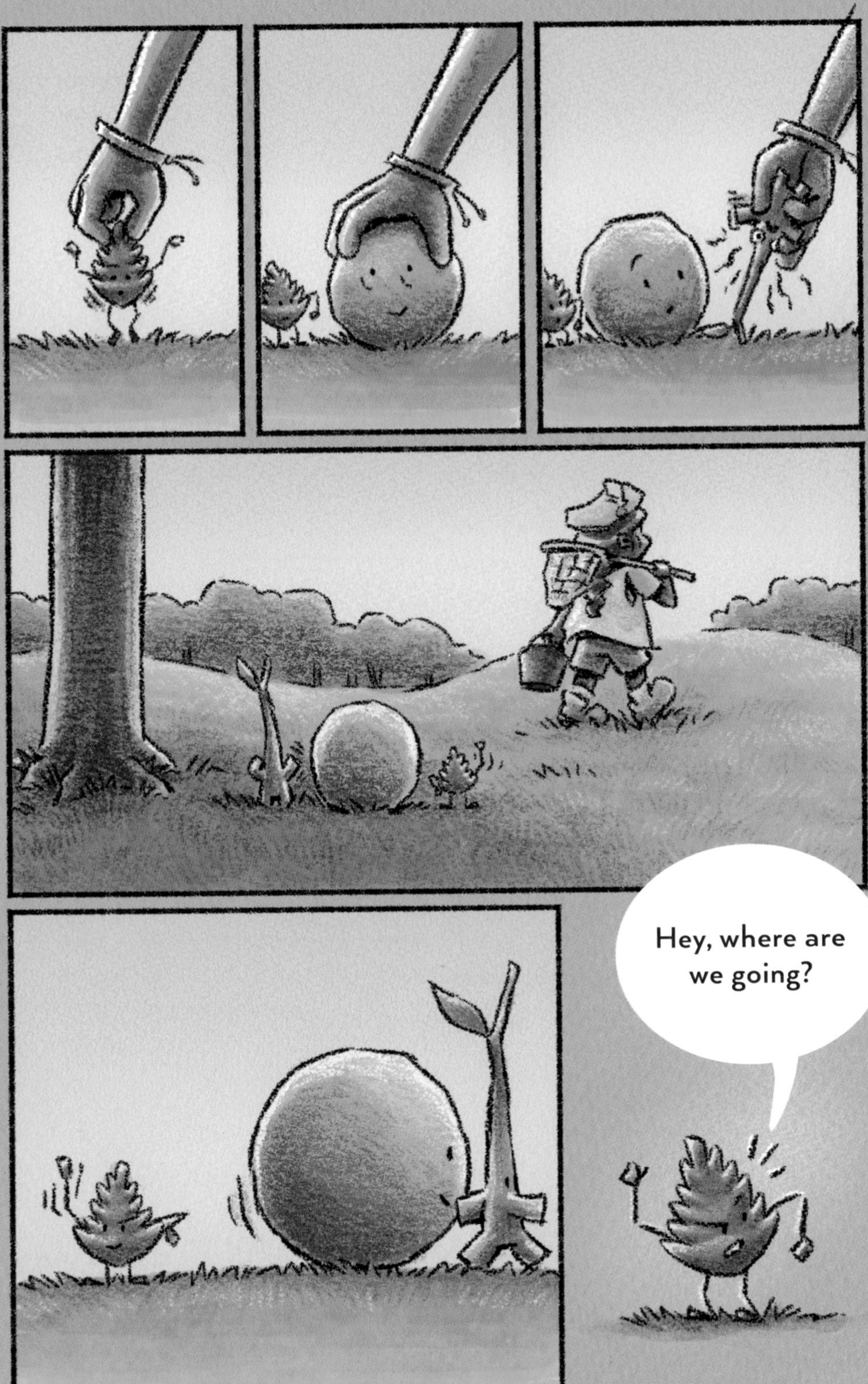
Hey, where are
we going?

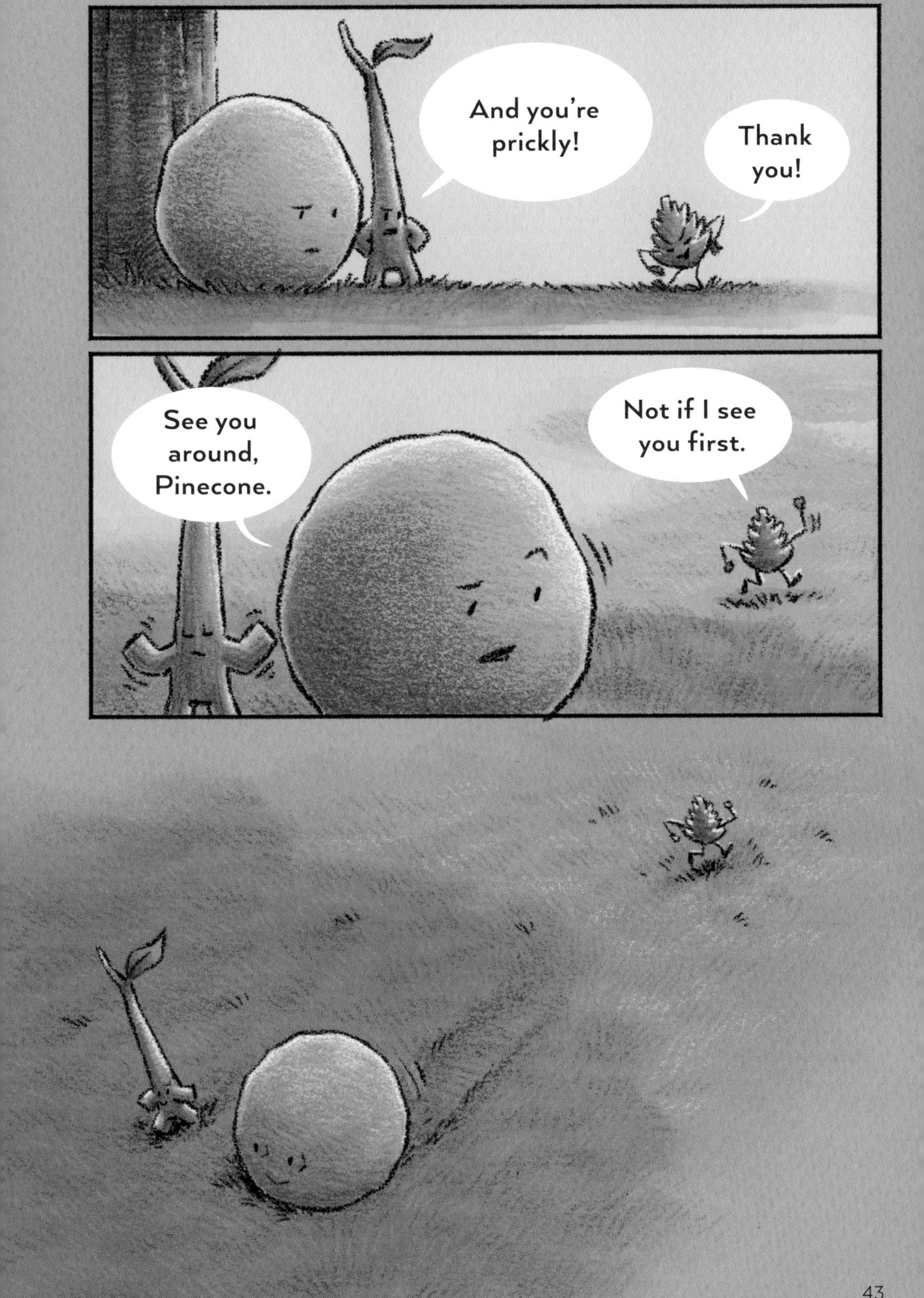

And you're prickly!
Thank you!
See you around, Pinecone.
Not if I see you first.

The Nature Girl's A–Z Checklist

How many can YOU find?

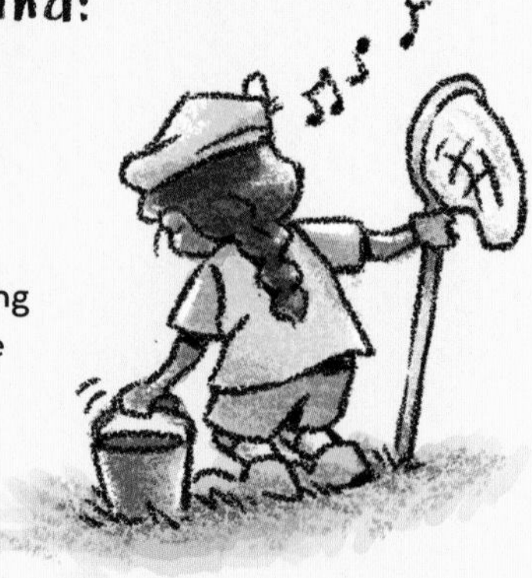

A Acorn • Animal tracks • Ants • Ant hills • Algae

B Beetle • Berries • Bees • Bark • Butterfly

C Clover • Creek bed • Cocoon • Caterpillar • Clouds • Cricket

D Dandelion • Dirt • Daffodil • Dogwood • Dragonfly • Dew

E Egg • Elm tree • Eagle • Egret • Erosion • Evergreen

F Fern • Feather • Frog • Fish • Fungus

G Grass • Grasshopper • Grain of sand • something Green

H Helicopter maple seed • Honeysuckle • Hive • Holly • Hummingbird

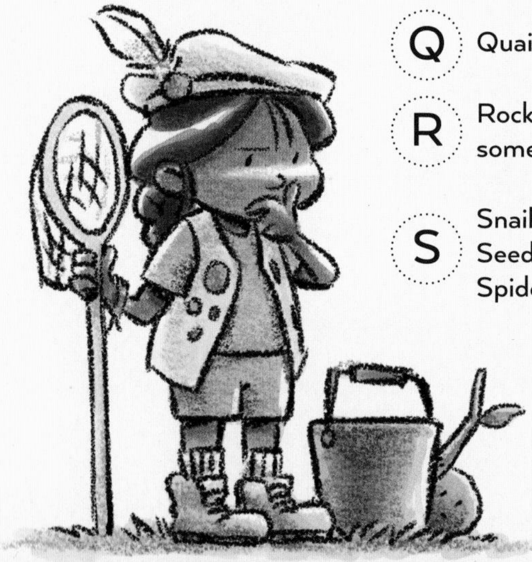

I Ivy • Inchworm • Iris • Insect

J Jewel weed • something Juicy • Jasmine • June bug • Jumping spider

K Kudzu • Katydid

L Leaf • Lily pad • Log • Ladybug • Lizard • Lightning bug • Lichen

M Moss • Mud • Mushroom • Mosquito • Moth

N Nest • Nut • Newt • Nettle • Nothing

O Oak leaf • Owl • something Oval • something Orange

P Pinecone • Pebble • Praying mantis • Pond skater • something Purple • Painted lady butterfly

Q Quail feather • Quartz

R Rock • Rose • Rabbit • something Red

S Snail • Stone • Stick • Seeds • Squirrel • Slug • Spider

T Twig • Tadpole • Tree • Toad • Turtle

U Unbroken branch • Underwing moth • Uniquely shaped leaf • Unusual rock • something Unexpected

V Vines • Vegetables • Violet • Valley • Viburnum

W Wildflower • Web • Worms • Weeds • Wasp • Wind • Wood • Wild Strawberry

X X-shaped twig

Y Yarrow • Yellowjacket • something Yellow • branch in the shape of a Y

Z Zinnia • Zero • Zilch . . . This one is a free pass if you need it!

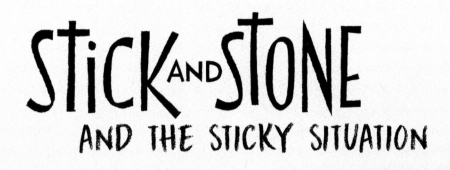

STICK AND STONE

AND THE STICKY SITUATION

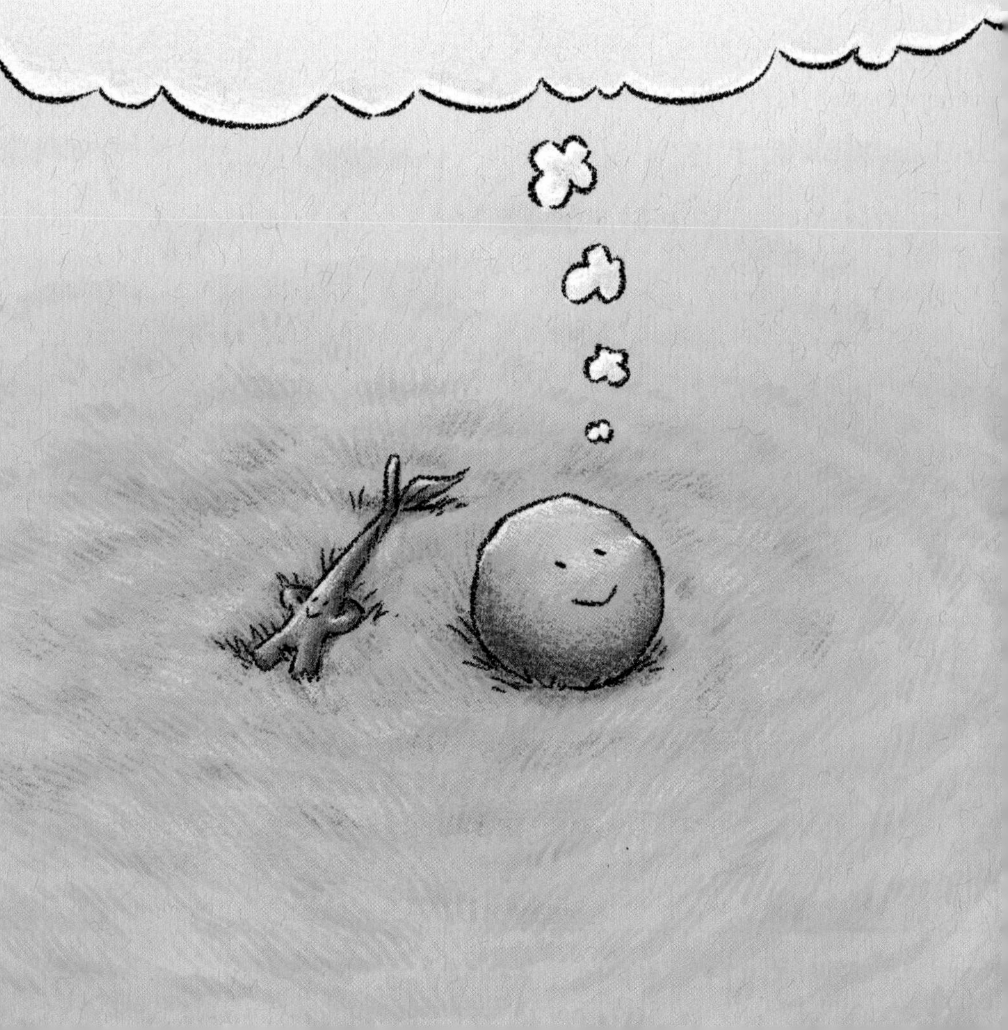

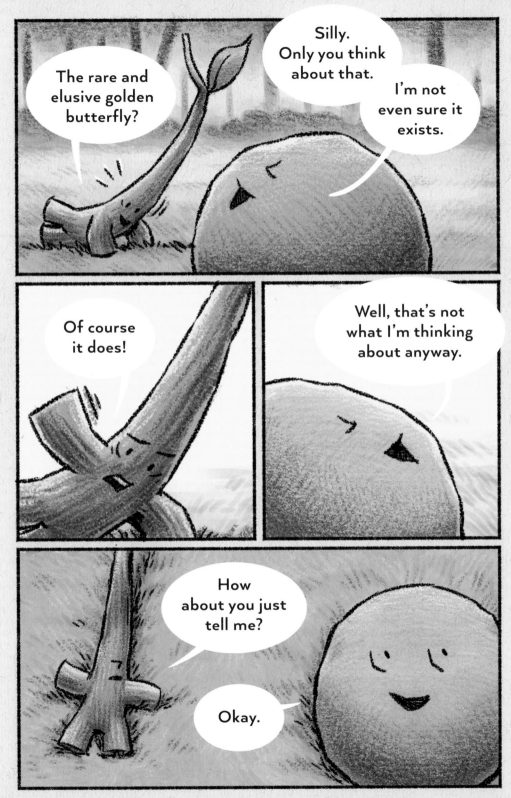

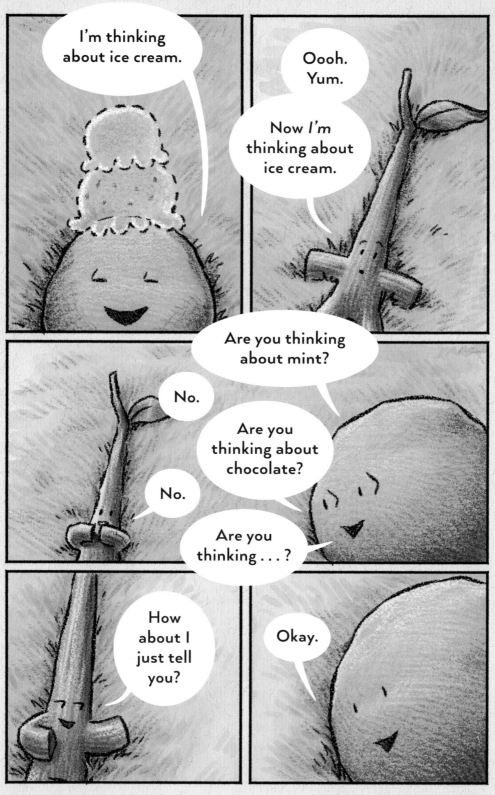

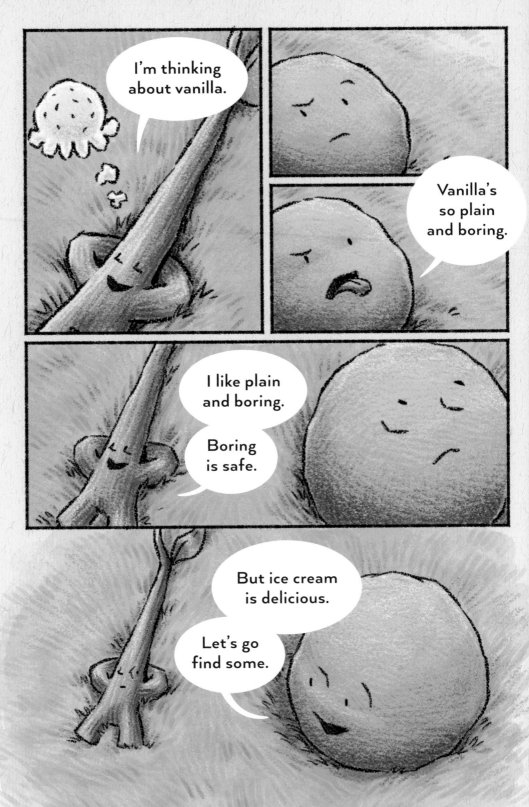

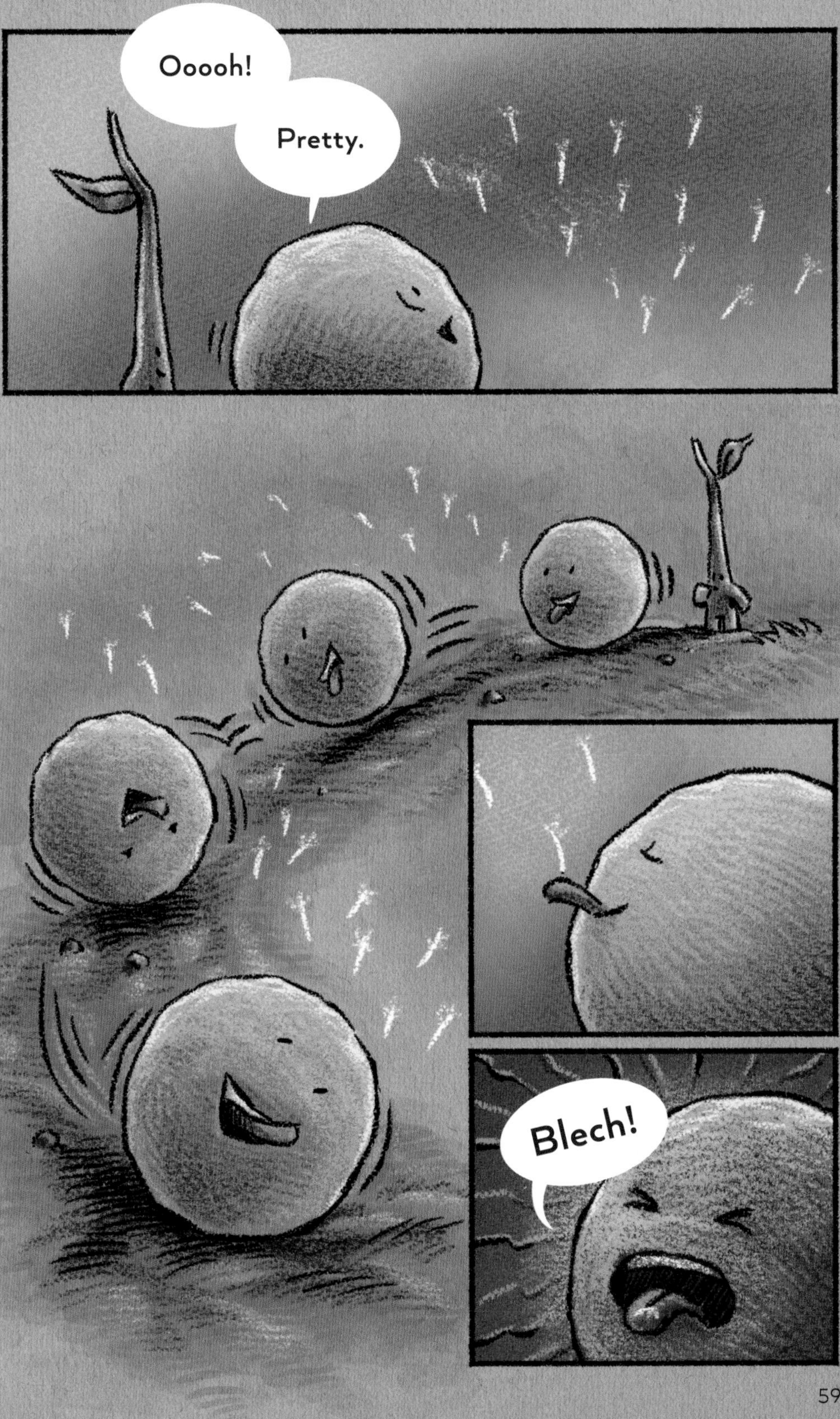
Ooooh!
Pretty.
Blech!

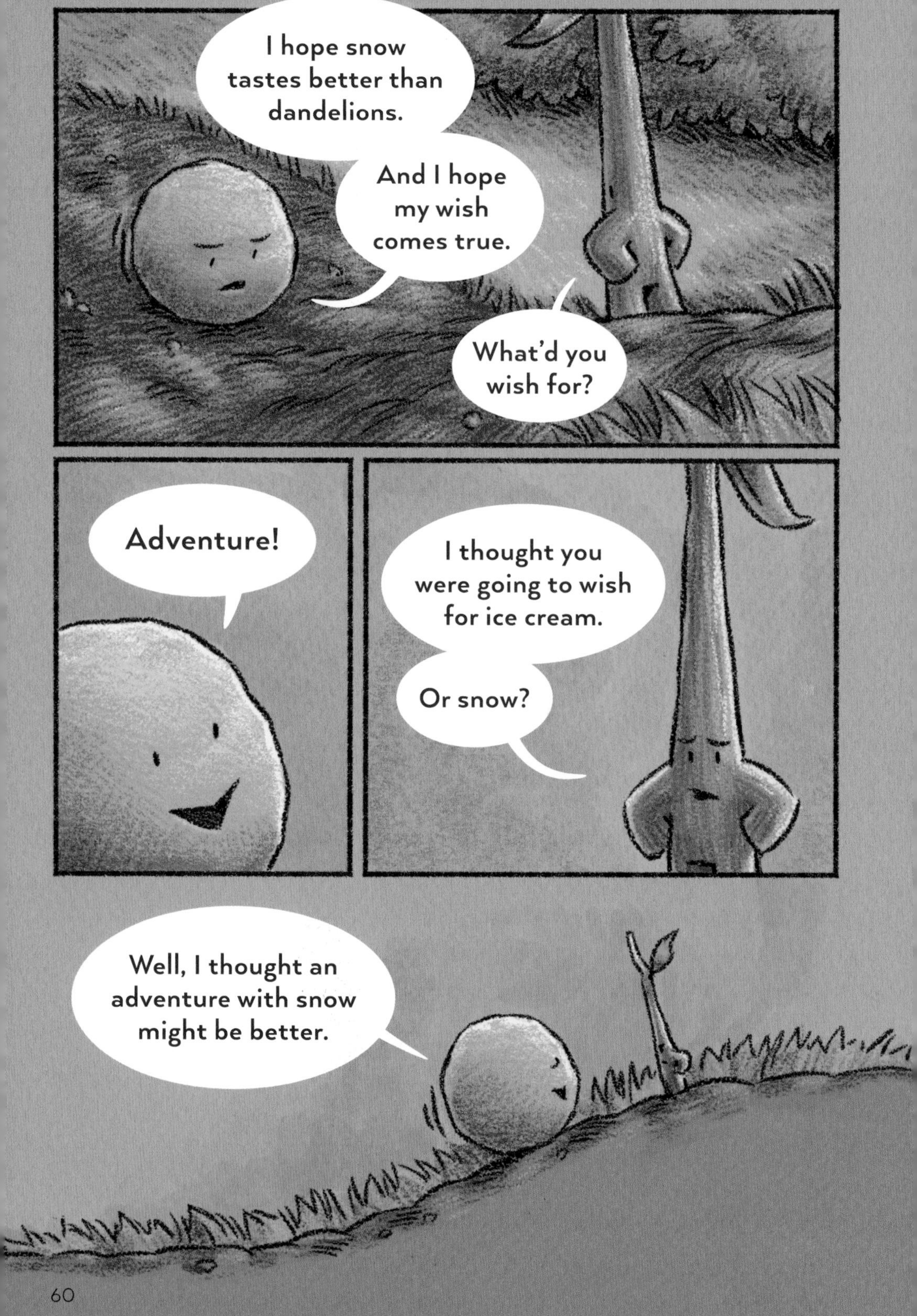
I hope snow tastes better than dandelions.
And I hope my wish comes true.
What'd you wish for?
Adventure!
I thought you were going to wish for ice cream.
Or snow?
Well, I thought an adventure with snow might be better.

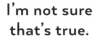

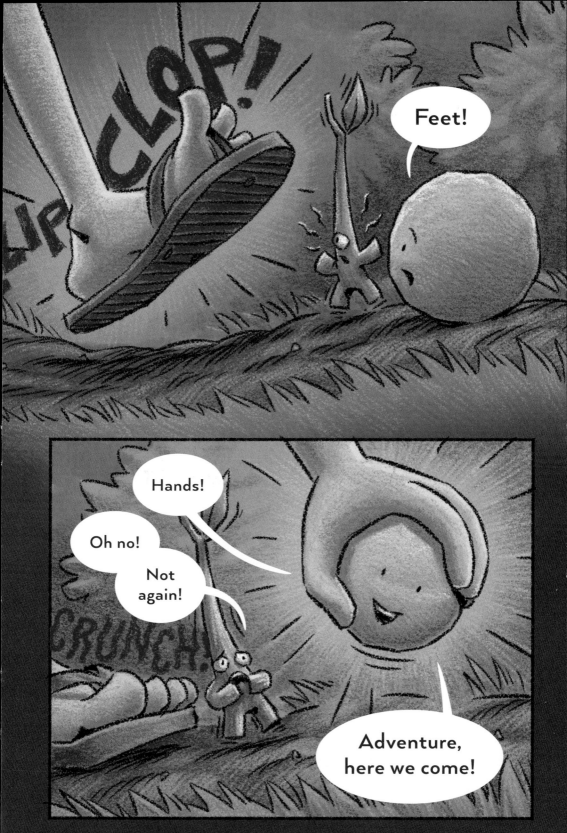

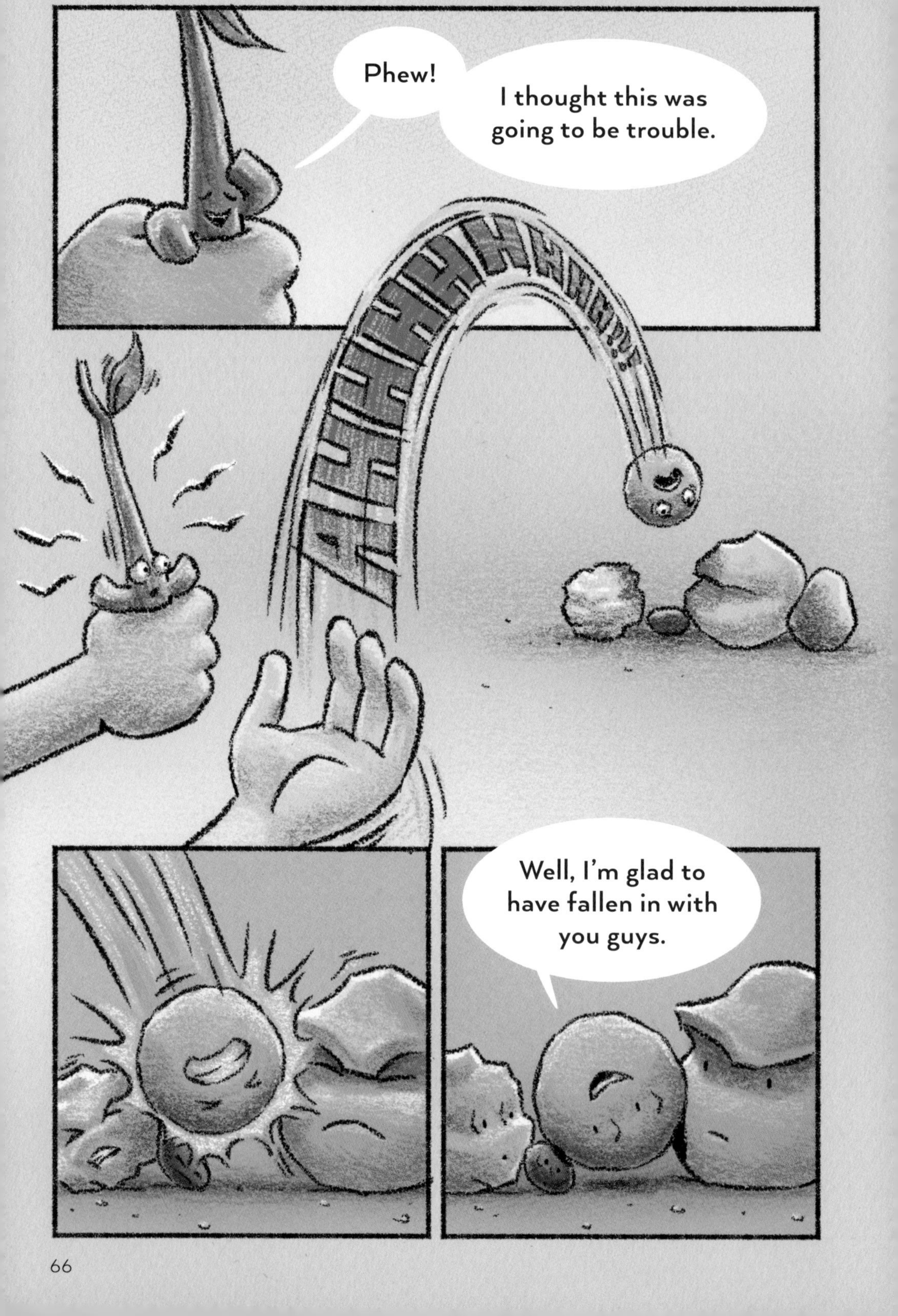
Phew!
I thought this was going to be trouble.
Well, I'm glad to have fallen in with you guys.

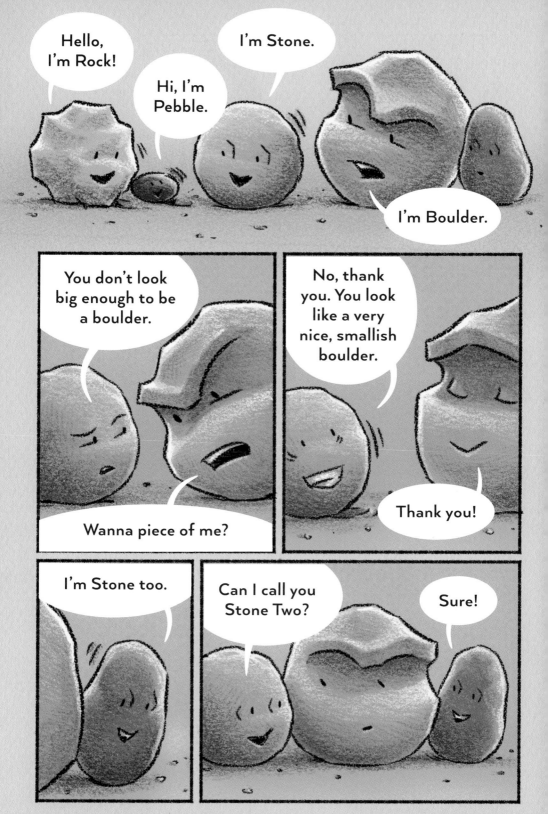

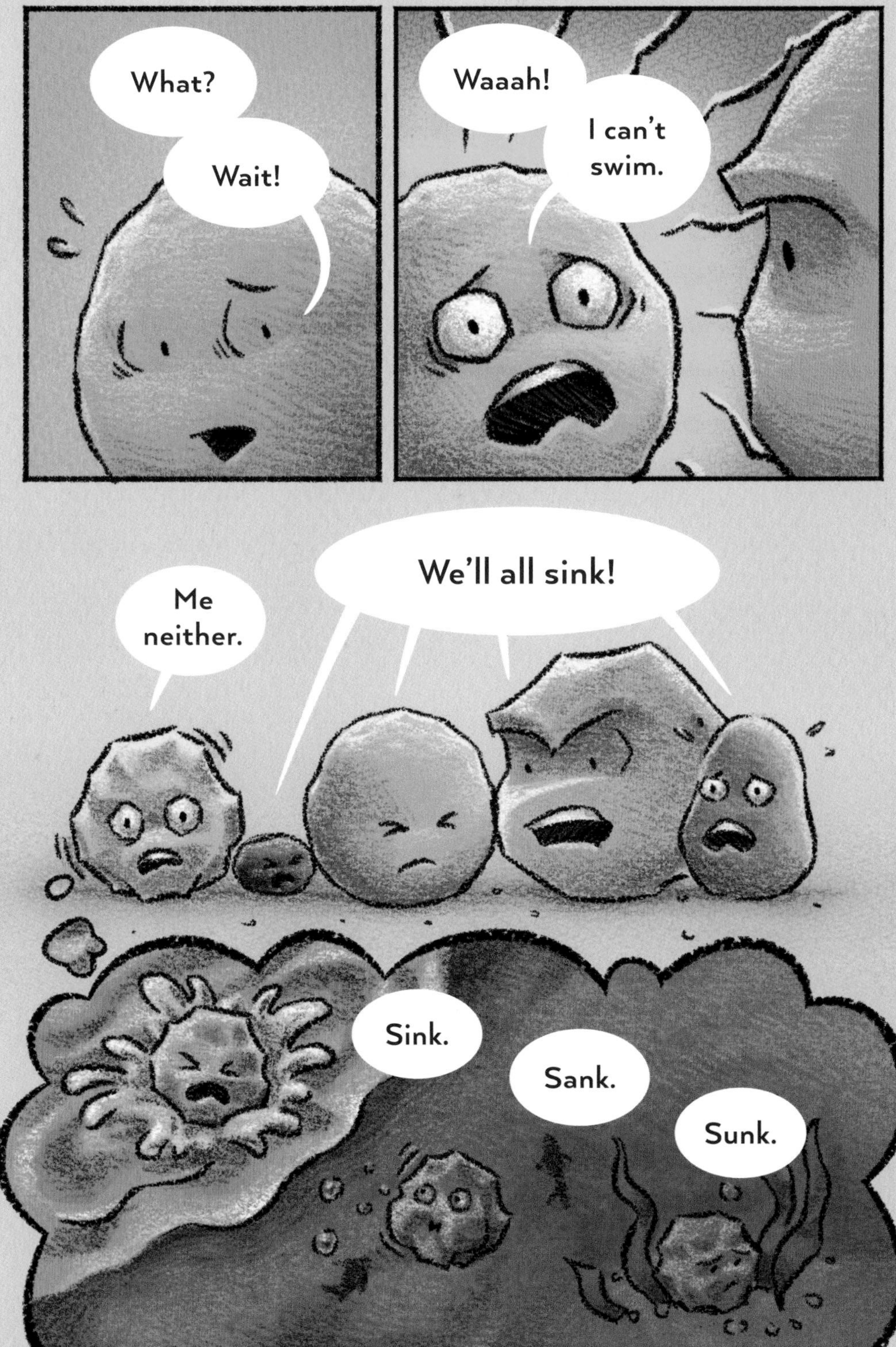
What?
Wait!
Waaah!
I can't swim.
Me neither.
We'll all sink!
Sink.
Sank.
Sunk.

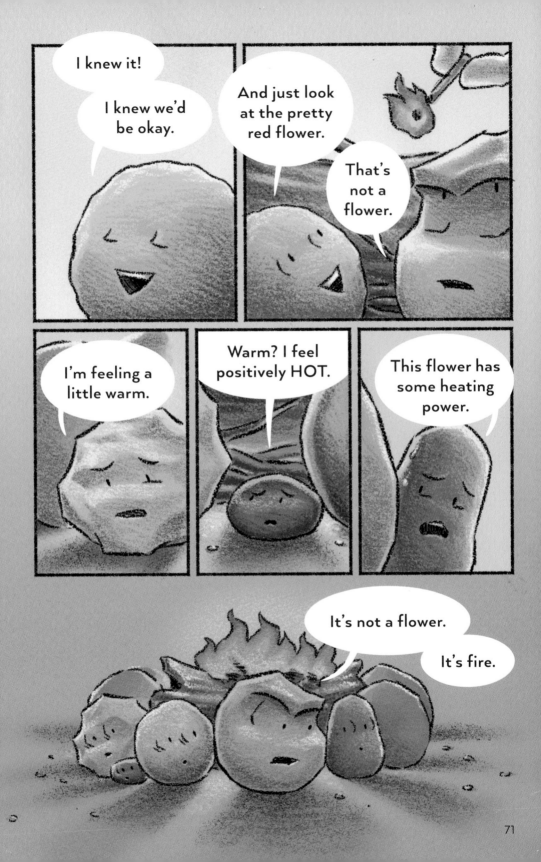

73

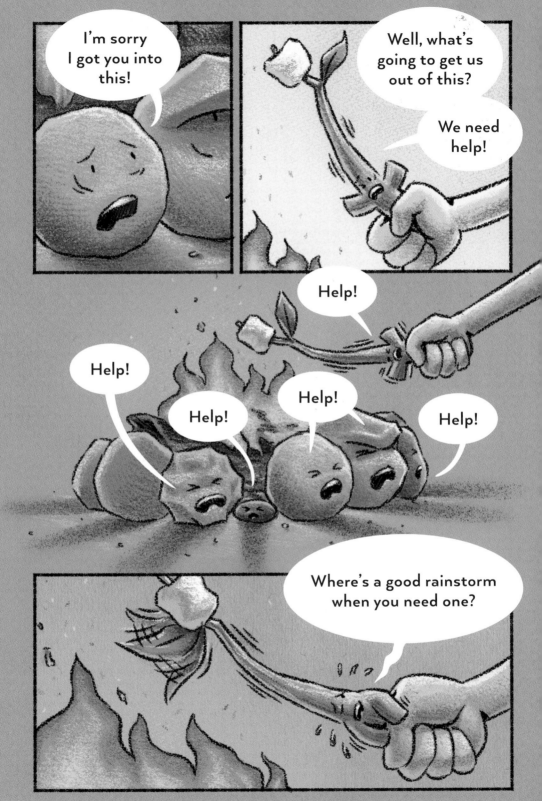

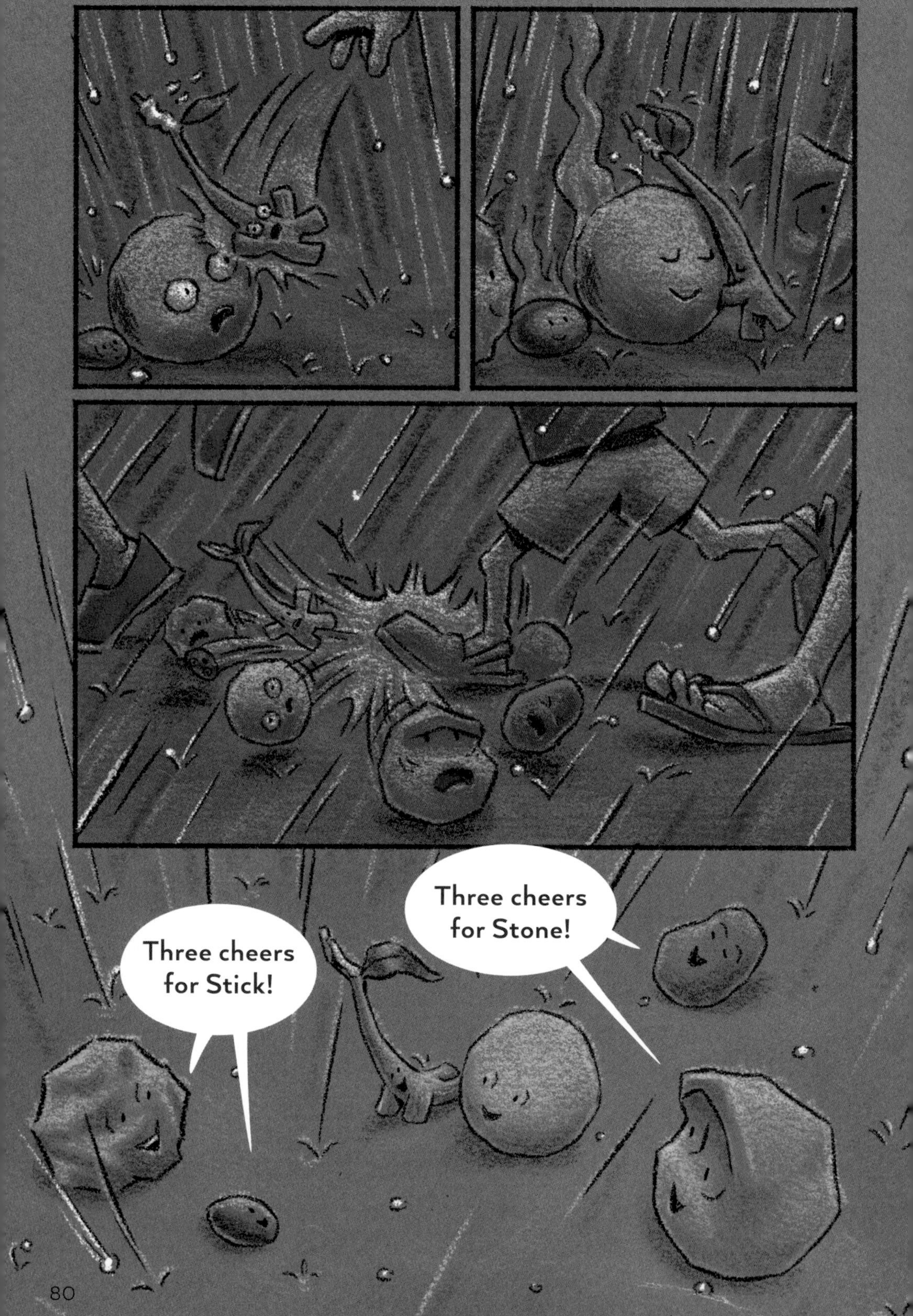
Three cheers for Stick!
Three cheers for Stone!

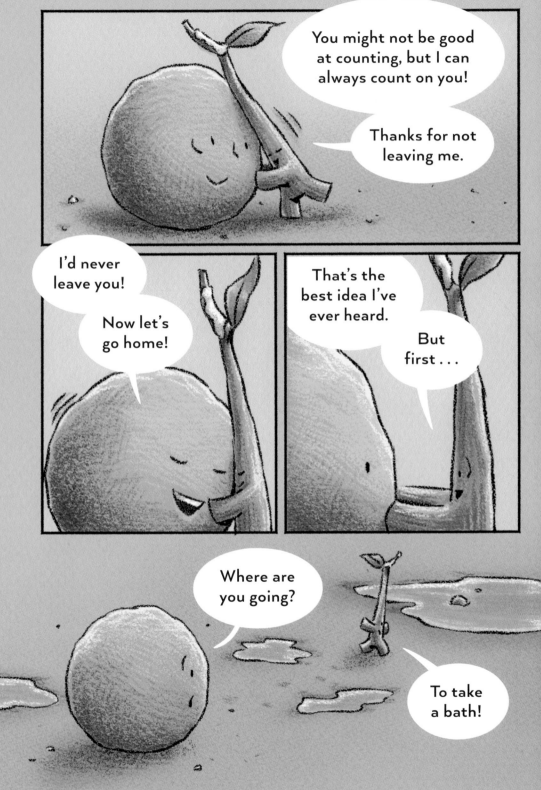

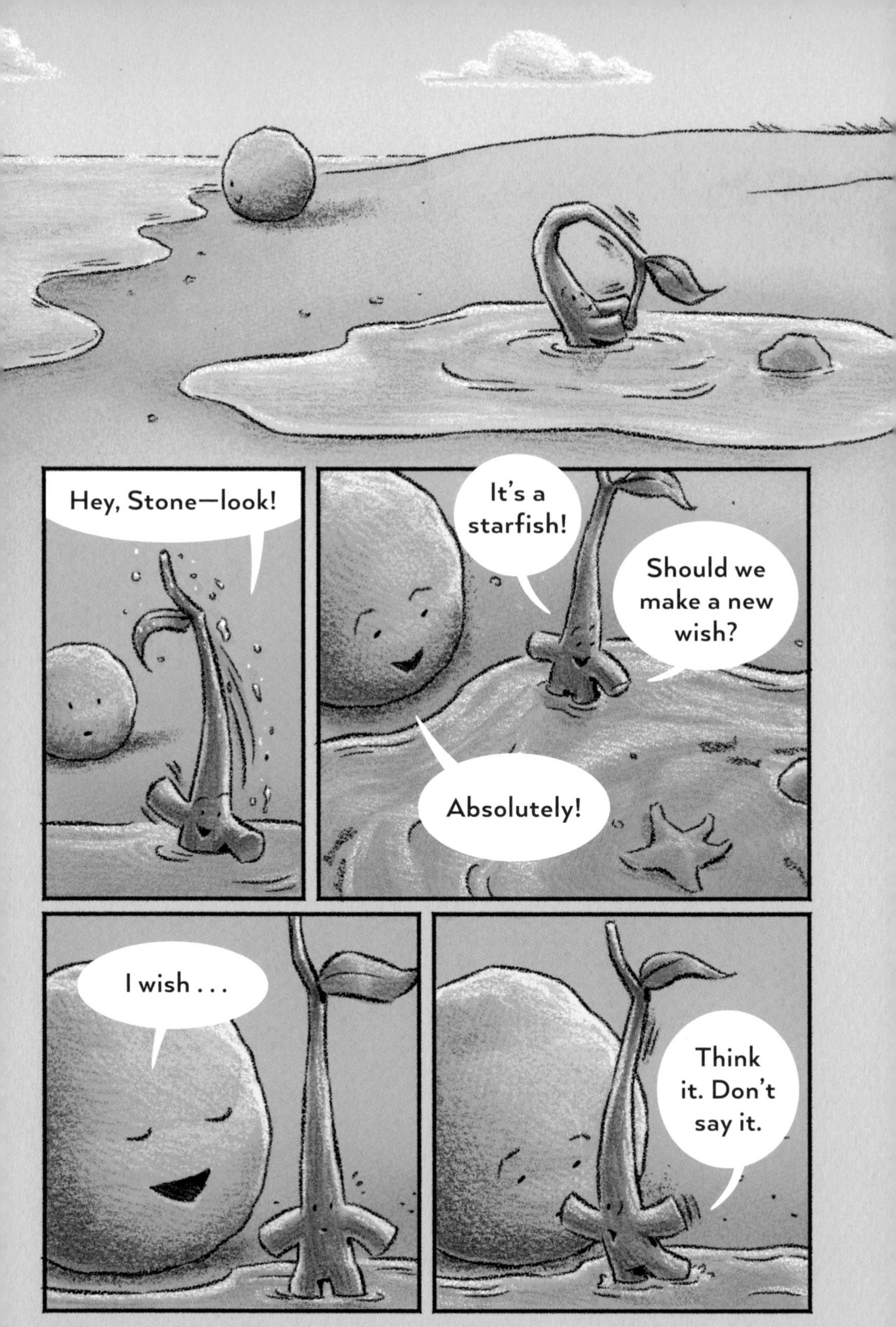
Hey, Stone—look!
It's a starfish!
Should we make a new wish?
Absolutely!
I wish . . .
Think it. Don't say it.

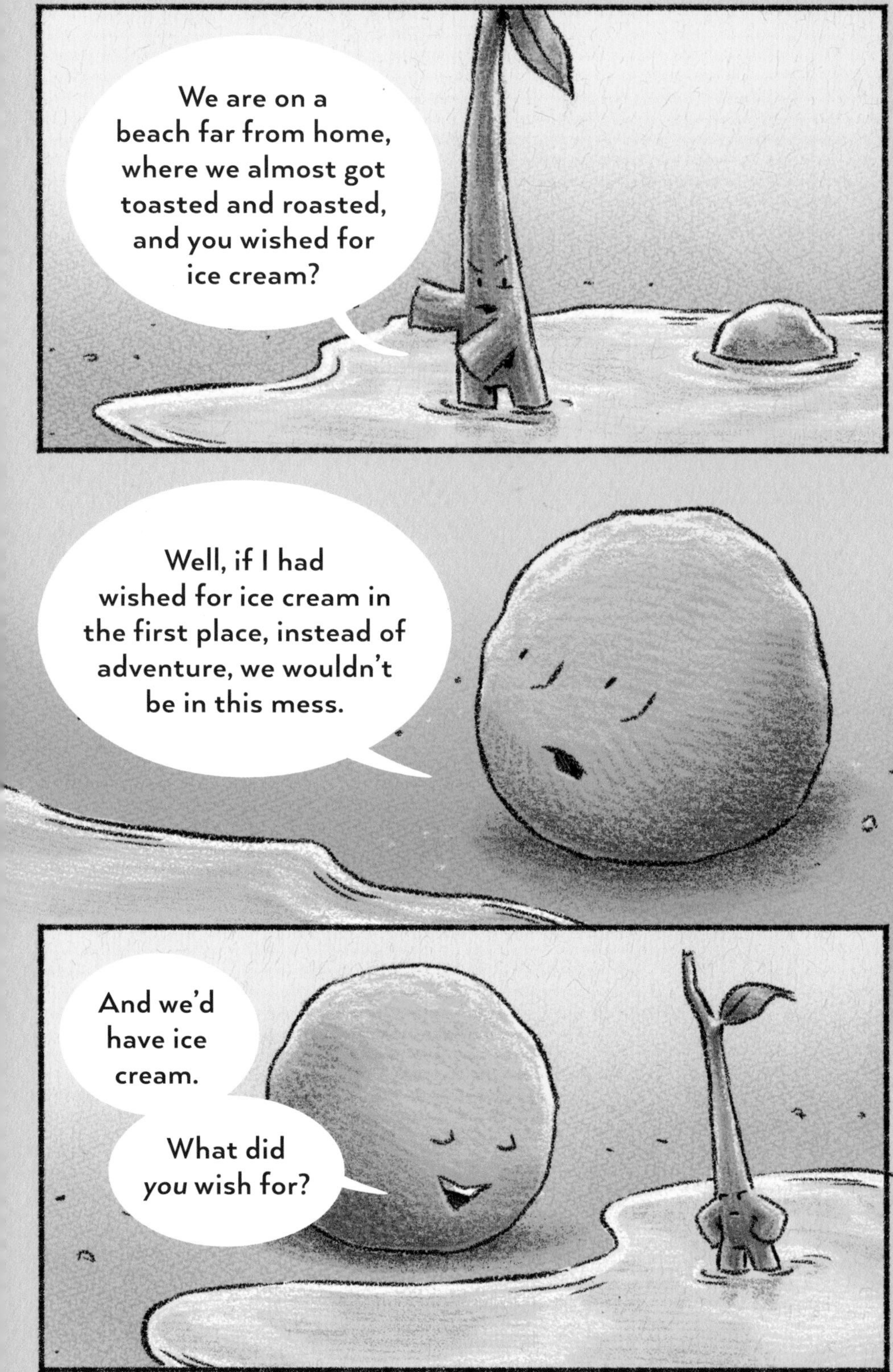
We are on a beach far from home, where we almost got toasted and roasted, and you wished for ice cream?
Well, if I had wished for ice cream in the first place, instead of adventure, we wouldn't be in this mess.
And we'd have ice cream.
What did *you* wish for?

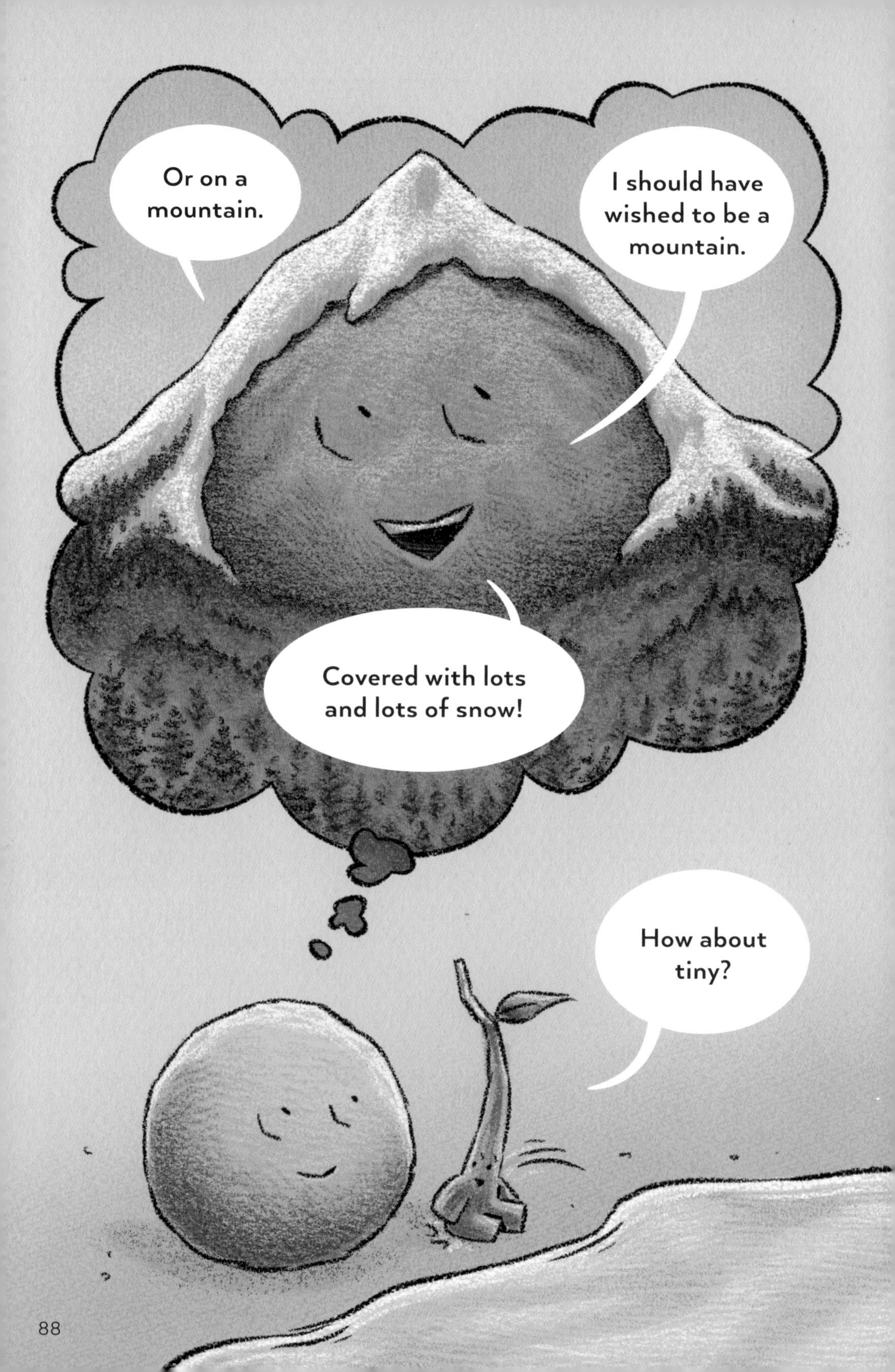

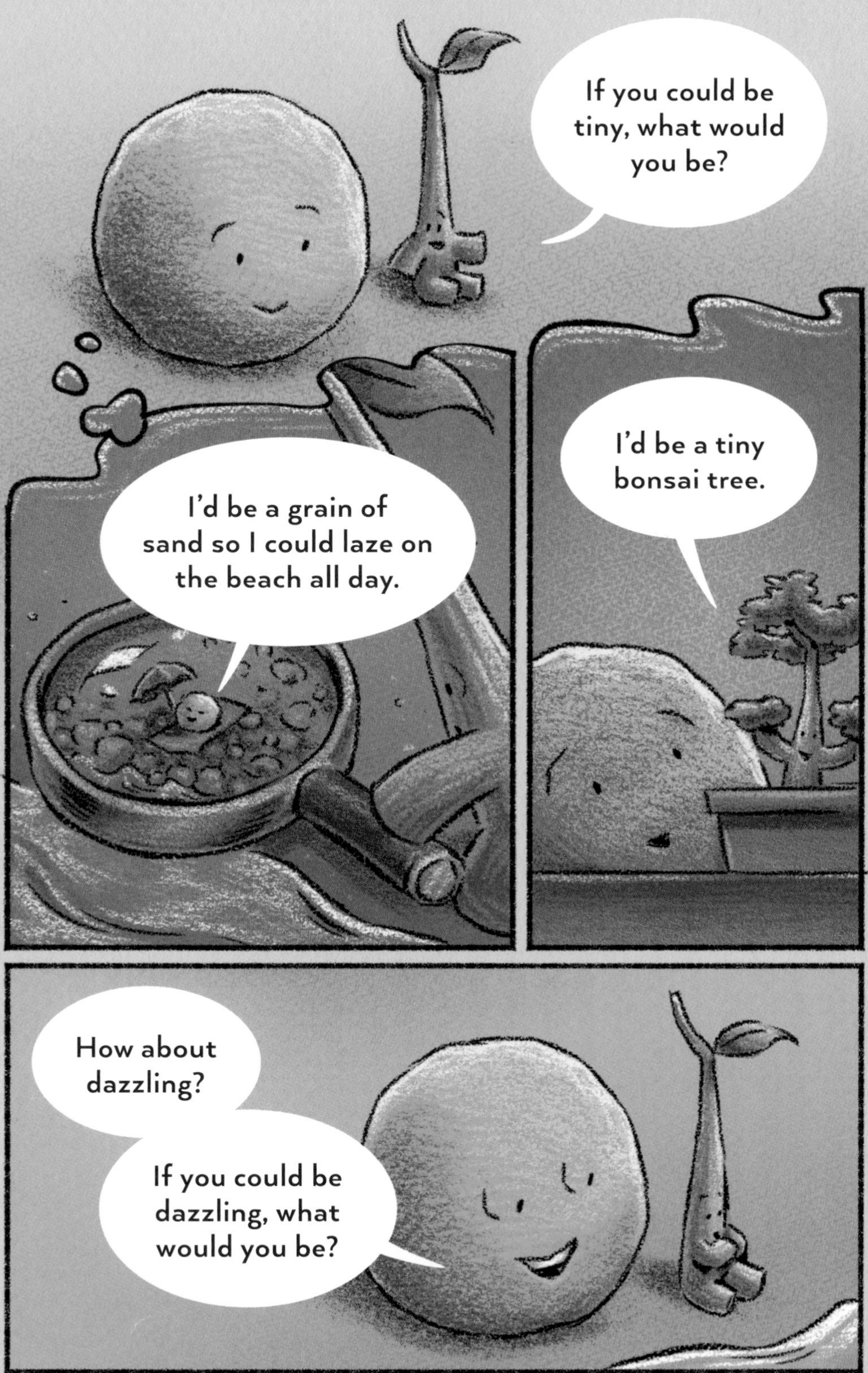
If you could be tiny, what would you be?
I'd be a grain of sand so I could laze on the beach all day.
I'd be a tiny bonsai tree.
How about dazzling?
If you could be dazzling, what would you be?

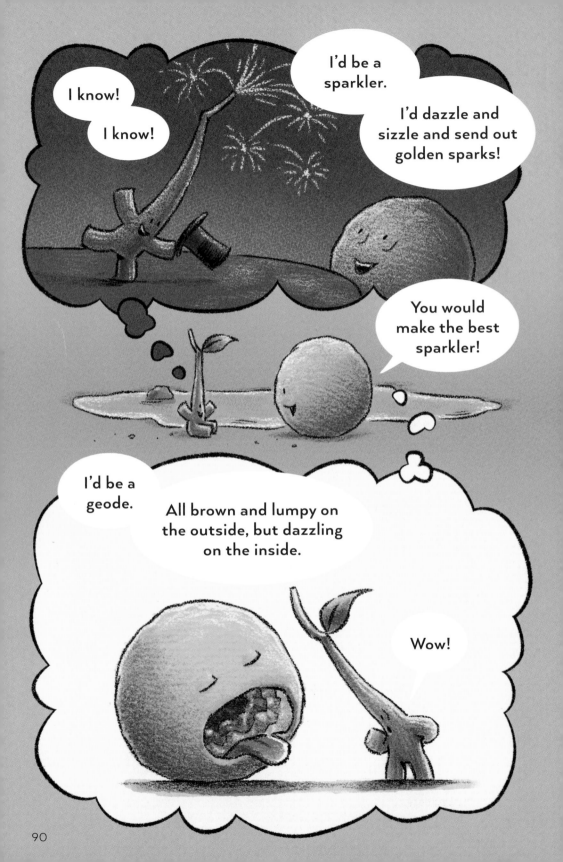

If you could go anywhere, where would you go?
I'd go to the Amazon and see all the rainforests.
I'd meet frogs and birds and butterflies.
Lots of butterflies.
Maybe even . . .
You wouldn't go without me, Stick, would you?
. . . the rare and elusive golden butterfly.

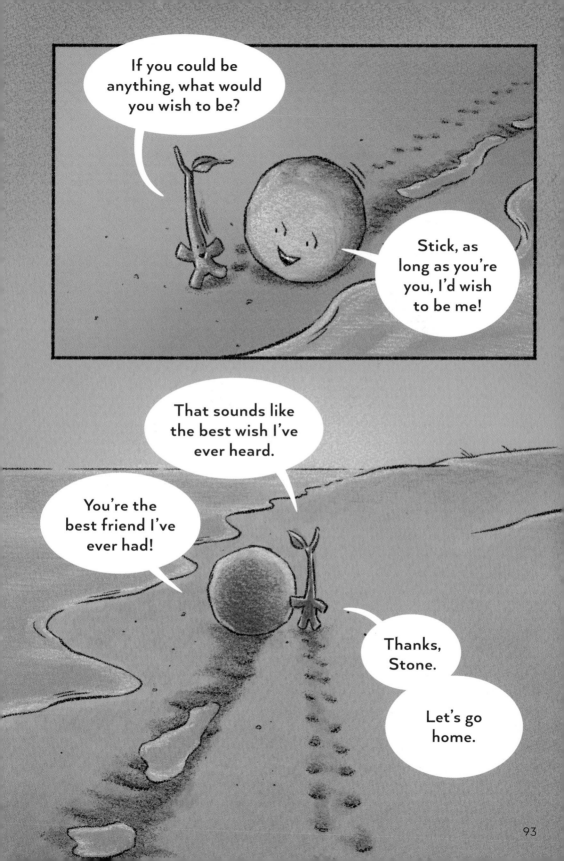

S'mores Recipe

SMOOSH!

Be sure to find the perfect stick!

Ingredients:
Marshmallows
Chocolate bars
Graham crackers

Traditional campfire method

- Place a marshmallow on the stick and toast till ooey-gooey.
- Slide marshmallow off the stick and onto a graham cracker square.
- Place a square of chocolate over the marshmallow.
- Top with a second graham cracker square and SMOOSH them together.
- Take a bite and then have s'more!

Oven method (makes many)

- Preheat oven to 350 degrees.
- Line a baking sheet with parchment paper.
- Lay graham cracker squares on paper, then top with a square of chocolate and a marshmallow.
- Bake 4–6 minutes, until marshmallow is puffy and chocolate is soft.
- Remove from oven and top with another graham cracker square and SMOOSH!

Microwave method (makes one)

- Place two graham cracker squares on a microwave-safe plate.
- Place a chocolate square on one cracker and a marshmallow on the other.
- Microwave for 15–20 seconds.
- Remove from microwave and flip one cracker on top of the other, then SMOOSH!

For Kate, who started this adventure and made every minute of it fun! —B.F.
To Mom for the encouragement, Tom for the opportunities, and both for their steadfast support. —K.C.

Clarion Books is an imprint of HarperCollins Publishers. · HarperAlley is an imprint of HarperCollins Publishers. Stick and Stone Explore and More · Text copyright © 2022 by Beth Ferry · Illustrations copyright © 2022 by Kristen Cella · Characters under license from Tom Lichtenheld LLC. · All rights reserved. Manufactured in Spain. No part of this book may be used or reproduced in any manner whatsoever without written permission except in the case of brief quotations embodied in critical articles and reviews. For information address HarperCollins Children's Books, a division of HarperCollins Publishers, 195 Broadway, New York, NY 10007. · www.harperalley.com · ISBN 978-0-358-54936-9 · The artist created the digital illustrations for this book with a drawing tablet, using brushes simulating pencils and watercolors and scans of drawing paper. · Typography by Alice Wang and Michelle Cunningham · 22 23 24 25 26 EP 10 9 8 7 6 5 4 3 2 1 · First Edition